KV-731-384

Border Savage

Savage's orders were to protect Mark Channing, the XL rancher, but he found out too late that Channing was a hated man. So when Channing was killed, Savage rode south in pursuit of El Lobo, the man Channing had feared above all others.

However, things turned out very differently from what he expected. He met El Lobo and survived, but faced even greater danger from Rodrigo of the Rurales, a man noted for his brutality.

It looked as if Savage had come to the end of the road. Before unmasking a cunning murderer he must first stay alive.

By the same author

Vermilion Springs' Vendetta
A Man Called Savage
Savage's Feud
The Savage River

Border Savage

SYDNEY J. BOUNDS

A Black Horse Western

ROBERT HALE · LONDON

© Sydney J. Bounds 2004
First published in Great Britain 2004

ISBN 0 7090 7456 5

Robert Hale Limited
Clerkenwell House
Clerkenwell Green
London EC1R 0HT

The right of Sydney J. Bounds to be identified as
author of this work has been asserted by him
in accordance with the Copyright, Designs and
Patents Act 1988.

DERBYNIWYD/ RECEIVED	6 MAY 2005
CONWY	
GWYNEDD	
MÔN	
COD POST/POST CODE	LL55 1AS

Typeset by
Derek Doyle & Associates, Liverpool.
Printed and bound in Great Britain by
Antony Rowe Limited, Wiltshire

CONTENTS

1	The Grey Ghost	7
2	Not Wanted in Eden	17
3	A Shot at Twilight	27
4	Dead Man's Legacy	37
5	South of the Border	45
6	Five Gold Coins	54
7	The Dog Trainer	66
8	The Siesta Raid	74
9	The Whip Hand	84
10	Ambush	92
11	Mexican Fandango	101
12	Return to Eden	111
13	Caesar's Nose	124
14	A Matter of Loyalty	133
15	A Daughter of El Lobo	144
16	Final Performance	149

CHAPTER 1

THE GREY GHOST

'You there! Stop where you are!'

Savage reined back his horse at the shout and sat waiting for the three horsemen to reach him. He waited patiently, relaxed, satisfied that he must be close to his destination.

He had an extensive view of rangeland that stretched for miles, a range that was quite possibly as large as a small country. Distant, he saw low hills and shallow valleys with clumps of stunted trees. In a cloudless sky, a hot sun hung like a disc of molten brass. Grazing cattle could be numbered in hundreds and their slow drift indicated where there was water. Somewhere there would be a ranch house.

The man leading the trio of riders had a weathered face beneath a flat black hat, and a single revolver holstered at his hip. The other two carried rifles and diverged, one to each side, bracketing him.

'This is XL land you're on, stranger.'

Savage said, 'Then I guess you can point me in the right direction for Mr Channing.'

One of the riders muttered, 'A Yankee.'

Their leader scowled, and corrected him.

'A damned Yankee!' He returned his attention to Savage. 'I could direct you, but why should I? It depends if you have a convincing reason. I'm Wilson, Mr Channing's foreman, so what's your business with the boss?'

He spoke with a Southern accent that was filled with suspicion.

'Your boss wrote to the Pinkerton office at Fremont for an agent, and I'm the one who got the job.'

'You figure us Texans can't look after the boss? Figure you can fight better than we can?'

Savage was aware of the other two riders closing in, crowding him.

'Looks to me like three to one.'

Wilson gave him a cold stare and laughed abruptly.

'Any Texan can whip three· Yankees single-handed any day!'

'Then it's a pity I didn't bring another two with me.'

'Suppose you get off'n that horse and show us what you can do?' the foreman challenged, sliding to the ground. He removed his hat and gunbelt and stood waiting. He was an older man, lean and hard, obviously experienced.

Savage sighed. This was not an ideal way to introduce himself to the XL crew, but he didn't seem to have much choice. He dismounted and hung his Stetson and Bowie knife on his saddle horn.

'He's only a kid,' one of the riders commented.

Savage's lips twitched in a smile, and he waited. As a dockside orphan he knew about rough-and-tumbles and he didn't doubt he was faster on his feet than the foreman. He also had a recent memory of Mary-Ann, a wrestler's woman who'd devastated him with a few throws.*

Savage was a quick learner; he'd spent time analysing her throws and stored away this new knowledge. Now he had the chance to try out what he'd learnt on someone else.

'What you waiting for, Yank?'

Wilson didn't wait. He balled his hands and rushed in, swinging. Savage caught the leading wrist in both hands and fell backwards, dragging the foreman after him. Wilson sailed clear over his head and landed in a heap on dry, hard-baked earth.

Savage was on his feet quickly. The two XL riders appeared to be stunned.

Their foreman lay motionless for a long moment, taken by surprise. When he'd got his wind

See *The Savage River*, Robert Hale, 2003.

back, he scrambled upright and rushed to attack again.

For a second time, Savage caught a wrist and threw him. This time Wilson was not so quick to recover. He glared up, spitting dirt from his mouth.

'Call that fighting? I'll show you how Texans do it.'

He lumbered upright and advanced slowly. Savage remained calm and let him come. Suddenly the foreman lashed out with a boot. Savage caught it in both hands, and twisted, and Wilson went down with a yelp of pain.

After this bone-bruising fall, he was seeing red. He staggered upright, wobbling on a damaged ankle. He wanted to break this Yankee kid into small pieces, and lunged with clawed hands.

Savage imprisoned an arm and pivoted on his heels, swinging Wilson off his feet and whirling him around like a stone in a sling. He released him without warning and the XL foreman went stumbling headlong until he collapsed.

He was still on the ground, and furious, when he gasped:

'Are you two going to sit there and let him get away with this?'

Savage shifted his gaze to the XL hands, but they were looking across the range. He turned to see a solidly built man wearing a coat and Stetson approaching on a grey stallion. A strong voice demanded:

'What's going on, Willy.'

Wilson scrambled to his feet, brushing dust from his clothes. His face was flushed and he was short of breath.

'A Yankee, boss – claims he's from Pinkerton's.'

'And you pulled your usual trick on an unsuspecting Northerner?'

One of the crew laughed.

'It was Willy who didn't suspect a thing this time, boss.'

Channing transferred his attention to Savage. 'You have proof of your claim, I suppose?'

Savage brought an envelope from his shirt pocket and handed it over. Channing tore it open and scanned the few lines inside; his gaze settled arrogantly on Savage.

'It looks all right.'

Wilson's face darkened in a scowl.

'Boss, we don't need help from any Yankee.'

'I guess you don't, Willy, when it comes to handling clodhoppers and townies. This is something else. Come with me, Savage.'

Savage put on his hat, climbed into the saddle and followed after his new employer.

Channing lifted an arm and pointed.

'That way lies the Rio Grande and, across the river, Mexico. I don't trust any greaser – a treacherous lot – so I need you to watch my back.'

As Savage raised an eyebrow, Channing continued:

'It's after dark when there's liable to be action. Someone took a shot through a lighted window and scared my wife.' Channing turned his head to look straight at him. 'That's your job, to stop this backshooter.'

They rode through the hot dry air in silence, Savage feeling satisfied that his wounds had finally healed. Dave Bridger, his supervisor, had insisted he rest after tangling with river pirates on the Missouri. It was comforting to know he was fit enough to handle Wilson.

Eventually he saw the XL ranch set low down in a hollow; the house was large and built of timber, with a roof that sloped gently to a parapet. To one side was the bunkhouse, on the other side a corral.

Channing dismounted and handed the reins to a bow-legged man.

'You'll have a room in the house,' he told Savage. 'Come in and meet my wife.'

He went up three steps to a veranda and pushed open the door. 'Gladys! Here!'

A big-boned woman appeared without hurry; she was past her best, her skin roughened by the climate.

'This is Mr Savage, a Pinkerton detective. He'll be staying with us.'

Savage murmured a greeting, thinking she'd been a looker once.

Gladys glanced at him, her face revealing nothing.

'Of course, he'll be for the Grey Ghost—'

'There's no ghost!' Channing almost shouted the words. 'Only a night-rider.'

12

She shrugged. 'If you say so, Mark. You have time to wash up, Mr Savage – there'll be a meal on the table in fifteen minutes. It's beef again, but—'

Channing snapped, 'There's nothing wrong with beef. Remember you married a cattleman!'

'You said a man could drive into town for supplies . . .'

'When we're not busy.'

Savage dropped his gear in a back room and sluiced under the yard pump. The meal was fine as far as he was concerned – thick juicy steaks with vegetables and chunks of bread – but Channing ignored his wife and monopolized the conversation. Mostly about his big ideas, his ambitions and his prospects.

If this is married life, Savage thought, he was glad he'd ducked out when that schoolteacher showed signs of getting broody.

The house appeared to be a home in transition; some of the furnishings were old and of quality; the newer stuff seemed shoddy by comparison.

Mrs Channing maintained a silence, a fixed smile, and behaved more like a servant.

After the meal, Savage thanked his hostess and escaped to collect his shotgun and get outside.

He walked around the main building until he found a window where the glass had been replaced; the repair was obvious. He followed the line of sight towards the open range and a slight rise; at night, a lighted window would be an easy target. To kill? Or just to scare?

13

'Reckon you're the Pinkerton.'

Savage turned to see the bow-legged man who'd led his mount to the corral: a slight figure, with a tanned dark skin and the wild look of a gypsy.

'Name's Henry, sometimes called Henry Horse, and I'm the wrangler for XL. You want to borrow a horse from our herd, you ask me.' He indicated the window. 'Can tell yuh the slug was shot from an old rifle. Come light, we followed the tracks till they were lost among cattle.'

'No ghost, then?'

'That's just talk, but this rider sure moved quick and quiet. Grey Ghost is a name that suits.'

'You have no problem talking to a Yankee?'

Henry's eyes showed a gleam of humour.

'I heard about Willy taking a fall. Waal, I don't take orders from him. I'm my own man, working directly for the boss.'

'Any idea who might be behind the shooting?'

Henry took out the makings and rolled a cigarette; he offered his pouch to Savage.

'Thanks, but I don't smoke.'

Henry lit up. 'The talk in town blames a Mex bandit, and the boss sure seems down on greasers. El Lobo's gang cross the border at times to steal a bunch of cows, but, by any account, he's big around the waist and needs a large horse to carry him. Not one to pretend he's a ghost, I figure.'

Savage nodded, thoughtful, and the wrangler went about his work.

He rested through the heat of day and, as dusk

hid shadows and lights were lit in the house, brought his horse from the corral and settled easily in the saddle.

Keeping to low ground he made an unhurried circuit of the buildings, listening, while his eyes adapted to the fading light. The sun vanished and there would be no moon for a while; by starlight, he watched the skyline for anything that moved.

The air was still and warm and he heard a cow calling her calf. Cloud drifted, reducing the light from the stars. Savage reined back, listening, waiting.

After a while he heard stealthy hoofbeats on the hard-baked earth. He turned his head, trying to decide the direction of the sounds; his horse, ears forward, pointed. Whoever was coming was moving slow and easy; small noises were muffled.

Savage slid from the saddle and crouched low, shotgun in his hands. The rider seemed to be in no hurry to reach the ranch house. Starlight brightened as cloud passed and his horse was suddenly revealed. The rider turned away with a sharp movement.

'Hold it right there!' Savage shouted. 'I've got you covered!'

The rider ignored his challenge, whirled about and kicked the horse to speed.

Savage mounted swiftly and set off in pursuit. He caught the barest glimpse of the rider, not enough to recognize him again, and cursed softly.

The unknown had a fast horse and was lying low

across the animal's back. Savage urged his own horse to a maximum effort, but the sound of the thudding hoofs of his quarry faded quickly.

Cloud dimmed the stars again and, when he could see clearly once more, he was alone on an empty prairie.

CHAPTER 2

NOT WANTED
IN EDEN

Despite Channing's instruction to watch his back, Savage decided his employer was safe enough with Wilson and his crew during daylight hours. So, after breakfast, he slipped away on his own and followed the trail across the range towards Eden.

It was a small town, snuggled into a bend in the Rio Grande. A muddy bank sloped down to the river which was narrow enough at this point for him to see its Mexican counterpart across the border.

He rode slowly down the dusty Main Street, passing saloons and stores and a few houses. There was a sprinkling of Mexicans on the boardwalks so there was at least some mixing between the two towns.

He saw a sign, TOWN JAIL, close by the bank, obviously closed, and called to a man sitting on a bench outside a saloon.

'Where can I find the marshal?'

The man jerked a thumb.

'At the smithy.'

Savage called, 'Thanks', and rode on, passing a butcher's shop selling mutton and pork and a wagon loading up. He reckoned the town marshal would know what was going on, even if his authority didn't stretch beyond Eden. He heard the ringing of metal on metal and followed it to a sign: DUTTON, LIVERY AND SMITH.

He smelled singed hair, dismounted and hitched his horse. There was a tattoo of hammer-blows and a shower of red and yellow sparks inside.

He walked into the dim interior where the smith was working; another figure lurked in shadow at the back; the marshal, maybe?

Dutton was squat and broad across the chest with powerful arm muscles, and wore a blackened leather apron. He finished shaping a piece of iron, doused it in a bucket of water and inspected the result. Then he looked up.

'You needing help, stranger?'

'I'm looking for the marshal.'

'That's me.'

Savage recovered quickly.

'You handle two jobs?'

Dutton studied him closely.

'The marshal's job is part-time, mainly locking

up drunks on a Saturday night.'

'I see you can handle those with no bother.'

Savage explained he was a Pinkerton agent assigned to the XL rancher, and asked:

'Does Mr Channing really have anything to worry about?'

Dutton's expression changed; it was no longer welcoming, and Savage felt he was being frozen out.

'I'd say he does. I'd say there are folk in town and the land around who hate the arrogant son-of-a-bitch. He's got money and land and likes to give orders.'

The marshal spat in the fire, as if to relieve his feelings, wiped his hands and started to fill a pipe.

'He's a grabber – anything someone else has, he wants. There's plenty who'd cheer if he stopped a bullet – shopkeepers, small ranchers, homesteaders. I just hope they don't kill him in town.' Dutton gave a short laugh. 'Sure's unfortunate, but you ain't going to head the popularity stakes if you're planning to help him stay alive.'

Savage shrugged.

'That goes with the job. Anyone in particular gunning for him?'

Dutton got his pipe going.

'Most folk place their bets on El Lobo – but don't ask me why a Mexican bandit should chase after him. Nobody has figured that out to my satisfaction.'

'Any trouble when the XL crew hit town?'

'Not till they've had a few drinks. By then, our Mexican visitors have disappeared – the men, that is. Their women are always welcome in some saloons.'

A slurred voice came from the shadows behind the smith.

'Let me tell yuh, feller, you ain't welcome here. You won't save Channing, if I have to shoot him myself!'

A thin figure holding a bottle swayed into view. It was male and had wispy grey hair, whiskers, and clothes that were stained and smelly.

Dutton spoke sharply. 'Quit that nonsense, Burt. I figure this here's a dangerous one.'

'So am I,' Burt mumbled, lurching forward.

Savage realized he was being braced by the town drunk, a no-win situation. He nodded to the marshal, and left.

Burt followed him along the boardwalk on Main, name-calling and howling a challenge.

'Stand and draw, Yankee. I'm the fastest and I'll run any hired scum of Channing out of town. I'll . . .'

Savage quickened his pace, heading for the hotel, reasoning that the management wouldn't allow this one inside. Men stepped off the boardwalk and women ducked into stores to avoid them.

'Stand and fight, you yeller dawg!'

Burt weaved an unsteady path, drawing everyone's attention. Savage compressed his lips, hands tightening on his shotgun. He crossed the street and went up the steps, watched by a group of men on the veranda. There were no friendly smiles amongst those drinking and smoking there.

Only one, dressed in new clothes in imitation of the West, seemed amused by the situation.

'It looks like you'll have to stand and fight, stranger!' the dude saide cheerfully.

English, Savage thought; the accent was a give-away. No doubt some relative of a wealthy family touring America and pretending he was roughing it.

'I'm the terror of Eden,' Burt chanted, following him up the steps. 'I'm going to show yuh how a Texan deals with a Yankee no-good. Or a dozen like you. Coming here to back up Channing, a nothing, a new boy in town . . .'

It was the word 'new' that made Savage pause, realizing how little he knew about Channing's background. He'd assumed the rancher was a pioneer from way back, almost a part of the land he claimed as his own, but if not . . . Assumptions were dangerous.

He stopped and faced Burt, took the bottle from his hand and threw it into the street. He pushed him into an empty seat and brought up his shot-gun to within an inch of his face. Even drunk, Burt knew what that meant if he pulled a trigger.

He sobered quickly.

'I didn't mean any harm—'

'Tell me about Channing,' Savage said. 'How long has he bossed the XL? Where did he come from?'

Burt stared into the muzzle of the shotgun and the ice-blue eyes behind it and began to babble.

'Not long, mister, and he bought the ranch—'

'Where did he get the money from?'

Burt turned sullen. 'How should I know?'

'Keep talking.'

'He came from nowhere and had the money to buy the biggest ranch in these parts. Now he tries to lord it over everybody.'

Savage remembered Gladys. Perhaps it was her money.

'Was he married when he arrived?'

'Her! She's just poor white and he's got plenty. She latched on—'

'Watch your tongue when speaking about a lady, Burt,' a townsman chimed in. 'And you, feller, with all the questions – nobody knows much about Channing, or wants to, except he's a bully and a bastard. And a braggart. Maybe you should just leave.'

There was a murmur of approval from the crowd, and Savage lowered his shotgun. He had enough to think about.

The English dude said quietly:

'May I suggest withdrawing to the dining-room, stranger? Allow me to buy you a meal.'

Savage nodded acceptance and followed him inside the hotel. It was only when they sat facing across a table that he realized the dude must be older than he looked. It was the fine fair hair and blue eyes that gave him an appearance of youth.

'My name's Lacey, and I'm from England, you know.'

'Savage. I guessed from your accent.'

Lacey called to a waiter.

'Steak, if you please, twice, and coffee.' He still seemed amused by the situation.

'It's hard on you, of course, but I don't believe the people of Eden are capable of distinguishing between you and Channing. And I suspect you're from the north, too – that won't help.'

Two large platters arrived filled with steak and vegetables.

Lacey continued; 'They dislike him, so they're going to dislike you.'

Savage hacked off a chunk of meat and speared it.

'Have you met Channing? What d'you think of him?'

'I've met Mark, yes – and I'm glad I'm not one of those who have to take orders from him. He's all business, all "I want". Back home, we try to be pleasant even when driving a hard bargain; we try to get along with people . . . but perhaps you take the same attitude as he does?'

'I'm from New York,' Savage admitted, but didn't mention it was the dockside he remembered, or that he'd been a thief who lived rough till Allan Pinkerton hired him.

'We do things differently,' Lacey said. 'Politely suggest an alternative over a drink . . .'

He used a toothpick to remove a shred of beef

from between his teeth.

'. . . try to be agreeable, meet difficulties half-way, accommodate small differences.'

They'd finished eating and sipped coffee. Savage was losing interest as the dude droned on. He recalled the English schoolteacher and wondered; were they all a bit strange?

'Channing bulls his way in and takes what he wants,' Lacey continued. 'Grabs would be a better word. He makes enemies and stirs up trouble for himself. All so unnecessary.'

The dude gave a little sigh, as if it affected him personally.

Savage said: 'If no one made trouble, I'd be out of a job.'

Somewhere close by a guitar struck a chord and went into a muted dance-rhythm. Savage found his feet tapping. Lacey pushed away his coffee cup and stood up.

'Come on,' he said. 'I'll show you it's not all trouble in Eden. Paloma is special.'

He went out by a back way and Savage followed, along a dirt path to the rear entrance of a saloon. Inside, tables had been moved back to make a space in the centre of the room.

In the mirror behind the bar, Savage saw the guitar player tucked away in a corner: a Mexican. He struck another chord, a cheer went up, and a dancer swept into the room with a colourful flourish.

She glided to the beat, sinuous, skirts swirling in

24

a froth of black and white and red, an off-the-shoulder gown revealing smooth olive skin. She swayed between the tables, smiling seductively and taunting the watching men, then bending away with a laugh. Her teeth gleamed white between vivid red lips, and long black hair flowed in waves.

Guitar music strummed faster and the dancer pushed a hip to her audience as she moved gracefully through a figure eight, heels drumming like castanets.

Lacey leaned close to Savage and whispered:

'Don't advertise yourself. She won't dance for Channing.'

Savage was in no mood to heed his warning. He was caught up in the music, blood pounding to the driving rhythm, following every move she made. The wild gypsy music excited every man in the crowded room.

Lacey was handsome and rich, attractive to women, and jealousy flushed through him.

The beat quickened again, her black veil and scarlet sash became a blur of colour. She flashed a show of olive leg, eyes sparkling and challenging.

She was a temptress whom every man wanted, and Savage edged forward, lured by her exotic beauty. She was the most exciting woman he'd ever seen and he wanted her. It was weeks since he'd bedded a woman and this one nearly drove him frantic. He wanted her *now*.

The guitar music reached a crescendo; the player struck a dramatic chord, and stopped.

Paloma snatched a red blossom from her hair and tossed it to the crowd. Eager hands grabbed for it.

In the silence, she faced Savage, staring him down, breasts heaving.

'Channing's dog,' she said, her lip curling, and spat in his face. Then she was gone.

CHAPTER 3

A SHOT AT TWILIGHT

'I'm telling you to stay close,' Channing said angrily. 'Your job is to watch my back, especially after dark. I don't want you running into town every five minutes, and I don't want to have to tell you again.'

The rancher was hatless, showing a bullet-head with close-cropped hair that made him appear twice as stubborn. Savage chewed and swallowed a piece of bacon before replying.

'If I nail this shooter, you'll have nothing more to worry about. To do that, I need to travel around freely.'

Channing snapped: 'I'm paying for protection, and you'll do what I say.'

It was not a cheerful breakfast in the XL ranch

house. Mrs Channing handed around more bacon from a pan.

'You won't change him, Mr Savage. I've told him we don't have to stay here – further north, that Mexican wouldn't be able to reach us.'

'This is my land, and we're staying! It's good land, I've a lot of it and I intend to expand. I'm aiming to be the important man in this part of the country. Wilson's boys can handle the locals, that's no problem. But this backshooter, sneaking across the border, is another matter. He's your job.'

'I'll stand a better chance of doing that if I can roam around.'

'No!'

Savage sipped coffee and swallowed.

'How sure are you that it's this Mexican they call El Lobo?'

'I'm sure!'

Channing got up and stamped out of the room, scowling. Savage lingered over another cup of coffee while Gladys Channing cleared the table.

She asked, 'Is Mark safe here?'

'I reckon so. There's a clear view all around the house, and his men are with him. I don't see a real risk during daylight.'

She nodded. 'It's a pity he doesn't scare easily – I don't fancy spending the rest of my life in this place.'

Savage drained his cup and walked outside. He circled the house, studying the ground; it was too

28

hard to take prints, but the dust would show whether anyone had sneaked close.

He felt restless. It was all right for Channing to give orders and put defence first; he didn't have to leave the ranch unless he chose to. But Savage had a need to act. He resented being kept on a leash, waiting for an assassin to strike; his nature demanded that he carry the fight to the enemy.

He wandered down to the corral where Henry was leading out horses for some cowhands. After they'd silently appraised him and ridden away, the wrangler said:

'I heard you tried to chase the Grey Ghost.'

'He lost me.'

'I don't doubt. You'll need a fast horse to catch that *hombre*.'

'Have you got one for me?'

Henry looked over the few horses remaining in the corral, and nodded. 'See that chestnut? He's a goer, but the hands don't want to work him because he grabs the bit and bolts.'

Savage looked over the chestnut stallion; the animal was tall and heavy-boned with long legs. There was a look in his eyes, set in an ugly head, that suggested a touch of the devil, but Savage now had enough experience not to worry.

'Sounds like he might catch this ghost rider.'

'If any horse can, Caesar will. Come in and be introduced.'

They stepped inside the corral and Henry carefully shut the gate. As he approached, the chestnut pricked his ears and began to nose at his shirt pocket.

'He knows I keep some sugar-lumps there. Nothing slow about this one.'

Henry pushed the horse's head away and dropped lumps of hard sugar into Savage's hand.

'You offer them – talk quietly to him. Let him hear your voice and get your scent.'

Savage held out his hand, dirty white lumps in the palm. Caesar sniffed; he was wary, but eventually gobbled the sugar. Savage ruffled his mane and whispered his name, and the horse seemed to accept him.

'Caesar will know you now,' Henry said. 'And he'll go like the wind if you let him.'

A cooling breeze stirred the air after the evening meal at the XL ranch house. Savage, shotgun across his knees, sat in a chair on the veranda, beside the rancher. From inside the house came small sounds as Gladys Channing cleared away the dishes. Ruder sounds echoed from the bunkhouse.

Channing sat with his back against the solid log wall, as usual. He was smoking a cigar and practising his lord-of-all-he-surveyed act; he was good at that, Savage thought.

The sun was taking its time to reach the horizon, turning the sky a flame-red; a few clouds drifted to cast moving shadows over the land. At moments like this, Savage could almost be glad he'd left city life behind.

He had saddled and tethered Caesar in a hollow between the corral and the house, close enough to reach quickly but out of sight. He didn't need another lecture from Channing when he wanted to get him to open up about his past.

'Why should a Mexican bandit risk crossing the border after you?'

His employer blew a smoke ring and studied it.

'El Lobo's a cattle-thief, among other things, and he wants what I've got. It's almost impossible to stop anyone slipping across and taking a few head. But if he thinks he can terrorize me into quitting, he's wrong.'

'But why you?'

Channing shrugged carelessly.

'Who knows the way a greaser's mind works?'

'It sounds more personal than that. Did you ever—'

There was a distant *crack* followed by a tinkle of falling glass. Channing swore and lurched from his chair into shadow.

Savage ran for Caesar, unhitched him and vaulted into the saddle. He kicked the chestnut's flanks.

'Go, Caesar!'

The stallion didn't need further encouragement; he was obviously glad to be free to run. The river, Savage thought, El Lobo would head for the border; and he aimed Caesar to cut him off.

In fading light he could barely see his quarry, but surely no horse could out-distance Caesar.

Long limbs flashed like pistons and hoofs drummed steadily on bone-hard ground. The light was going fast and Savage strained to catch a glimpse of whoever had fired the shot. The rider had a long gun but, if he got close, his own shotgun was the surer weapon.

As clouds blocked the starlight he imagined the gunman was veering away to one side, no longer trying for a river crossing. He seemed to be aiming for Eden.

Savage turned Caesar's head, and followed. The stallion responded as if eager to win a race. Miles fled by beneath a cloak of darkness and Savage hoped fervently that his mount wouldn't put a leg in a hole.

If El Lobo was the Grey Ghost, he had a good horse under him: Caesar was gaining, but slowly. In the darkness the oil-lamps of Eden gleamed ahead; if Savage lost sight of him now he might never find him among the buildings and alleys.

He reached town and raced the length of Main Street without seeing his quarry. The Grey Ghost had vanished as if he were a real ghost. Savage turned and rode slowly back, watching the gaps between buildings. He saw no one, and realized he'd get no help from the townsfolk. They were united against Channing.

He dismounted, tied Caesar to a hitching post and continued the search on foot, carrying his shotgun. There was a horse tethered in shadow beside the Shamrock saloon; he ran a hand over its flanks and found them damp with sweat.

He heard guitar music and knew where he was, pushed through the batwings in time to see Paloma reaching the climax of a dance-routine. His gaze raked the crowd of men watching her, but the only Mexicans in sight were the dancer and her guitar-player.

Paloma ended with a flourish; he forced a path through the crowd to reach her. Her smile faded.

'You again?'

Savage stared coldly.

'A Mexican just came in. Where's he hiding?'

She moved bare shoulders. 'I saw no one—'

'You're lying!'

A loud voice cut in: 'Is this feller bothering yuh, *señorita?*'

'How could he?' She tossed back dark hair and smiled. 'When I am among so many friends . . .'

She glided towards a door at the rear of the saloon. Savage started to follow her and suddenly found himself surrounded by men.

'Not so fast, *hombre.* I recall you were here before, with that dude.'

'Yep, and someone said he worked for Channing.'

Savage tried to bring up his shotgun, but hard bodies crowded close, limiting his moves. Bodies that smelled of beer or whiskey. Strong hands gripped, pushed and pulled. He tried to struggle free but was kept off-balance.

From behind the bar, a redheaded man called

in a thick brogue:

'No blood in here, boys. I don't want trouble with the marshal.'

'Right you are, Mike!'

Savage was disarmed and dragged towards the batwings and pushed violently. It was now full dark except for reflected light gleaming on whiskered and grinning faces.

Fists hammered him and he stumbled.

'We'll teach yuh to stay in Channing's kennel.'

A wooden club slammed against the back of his skull and he sagged, dazed. They let him fall and he curled into a ball as boots kicked his ribs. He tried to roll away and didn't quite make it. Sharp pain shot through him.

A fading voice said:

'We don't want Channing, and we sure as hell don't want you, so get outa town and stay out.'

A final kick to his head brought darkness and silence. He didn't feel a thing when they dragged him off the planks and dumped him in an alley.

The light was too bright. His head ached and his ribs hurt. Savage shuddered; daylight, so it must be morning. He tried to stretch and found he was lying on a bunk set against a wall. There were bars across the window.

He was in jail. Why? There seemed to be a gap in his memory.

Someone ran a heavy cane along the bars in the cell door before it opened. Dutton said; 'I let you

34

sleep late – now I want you out of town.'

Savage eased his feet to the floor, and winced.

'What happened?'

'You were found in an alley and I locked you up for your own safety. For a Pinkerton, you're sure slow to catch on.'

It was the first time he'd seen the marshal without his leather apron; solid muscle filled a check shirt.

Savage took a long deep breath and tested his arms and legs. Bruises, cuts, but nothing broken. His Bowie was back in its sheath.

'My horse?'

'I've got your horse, and shotgun, so listen, kid. Paloma is popular and that makes you a trouble-maker. I want you to leave Eden right now and, this time, stay away.'

Savage limped towards the door.

'I'm getting breakfast first.'

'Don't be stupid—'

An amused voice drawled:

'Stubborn, isn't he? I'll take him to the hotel, Marshal. He'll be safe as my guest. There'll be no bother.'

It was the English dude.

Dutton growled: 'Waal, make sure he leaves right after,' and handed Savage his shotgun. 'Your horse is at the livery.'

As they moved along the boardwalk towards the hotel, Lacey looked critically at him. 'Lucky you – I heard what happened. Lucky you can give our sawbones a miss. It seems he was an army surgeon and still favours cutting for most things.'

Savage paused at the Shamrock. Naturally, the Grey Ghost's horse had gone.

A few townsmen smirked as he limped past, but no one spoke. In the dining-room, he found his appetite hadn't been hurt at all; he called for a second helping of bacon and beans.

Lacey was apologetic.

'It's a pity I wasn't around last night – I might have saved you a few bruises. But as it happens, I had business of my own elsewhere. I'm sorry.'

Savage nodded absently, not really interested. If this dude assumed he was looking for help, he was wrong; he never relied on anybody else.

Maybe Lacey had been born with a silver spoon in his mouth and servants to wait on him, but he hadn't. He'd been a loner since his early days on New York's docksides, and able to look after himself.

But Marshal Dutton was right; there was no point in staying in Eden. He drank another cup of coffee and nodded to the dude.

'Thanks, Mr Lacey.'

Then he walked to the livery, collected Caesar and set off back to the XL.

CHAPTER 4

DEAD MAN'S LEGACY

The sky was blue and the sun climbing. Another scorcher, Savage thought, and let Caesar set his own pace; the grass was turning brown.

He was almost in sight of the ranch house when he saw Wilson and a few hands driving cattle, and assumed they were moving them to fresher pasture.

The foreman spotted him, left the others and rode towards him, his weathered face drawn into harsh lines.

'Where the hell have you been?'

'In jail.'

Wilson was taken aback for a moment, then returned to the attack.

'You'll need a better excuse than that. The boss

ordered you to stay close, and you deserted him.'

'I nearly caught—'

'You nearly caught . . .' Wilson's lips curled in a sneer. 'Waal, El Lobo did catch the boss alone and unawares. While you were missing, he sneaked up behind the boss and killed him.'

'Killed! Where were you?'

The foreman flared up. 'Don't try to put the blame on me! I've already told Mrs Channing it's your fault. We stayed with him till he dismissed us, and it was quiet enough then.'

'So what happened?'

'It seems the boss returned to the veranda to smoke a last cigar before turning in, and that's when El Lobo got to him . . . so there's nothing to keep you here and you ain't welcome at the XL.'

Mr Allan isn't going to like this, Savage thought, and said quietly, 'I'll see Mrs Channing first.'

'Maybe we ought to lynch you,' Wilson said viciously. 'I hope Pinkerton fires yuh!' He wheeled his horse about and rejoined his crew.

Savage rode on to the ranch and handed Caesar back to Henry Horse before going into the house. He found Gladys Channing in the office, staring blankly at a pile of paperwork. Her face gave no clue to her thoughts, though she appeared calm.

Savage removed his hat and held it in front of him. 'I'm sorry about your husband – the shooter got away.'

She nodded, not really seeing him. Her voice was low and he had to bend forward to hear.

'These things happen. At least I don't have to stay here now. What will you do?'

'My supervisor will expect me to bring in his killer.'

'Does it really matter? Nothing will bring Mark back.'

'Where is he?'

'They've laid him out in the hay barn. I can't imagine why – it's not as though any neighbours will come to the funeral.' For the first time, a note of bitterness crept into her voice.

Savage excused himself and crossed the yard to the barn, where he was joined by Henry Horse.

'She's a calm one.'

The wrangler shrugged. 'Still in shock, I'd say.'

Channing lay face up up on two planks supported by empty crates. He seemed to have shrunk; the skin of his face was slack and gave no hint of the power he'd assumed in life.

'Wilson told me he was knifed from behind. Is that right?'

'Right. We found him on the veranda, face down. The knife was still in his back.'

Savage tried to imagine the scene. Channing usually sat with his back to the solid wall of the house.

'Would you say he was a trusting man?'

A faint smile flitted across Henry's dark face.

'I wouldn't, no, and not where any greaser is concerned. He sure didn't like the breed.'

Henry reached behind him and held out a

knife; it had a slender blade, still stained, and a fancy handle.

'This is the one – typical Mexican work.'

Savage weighed the knife in his hand; light, but sharp as any razor, it would slide easily between the rib-cage.

He was puzzled. Everyone seemed ready to believe this was the work of El Lobo, and Channing himself had been sure of the identity of his assassin.

But a knife in the back suggested someone Channing trusted. Savage felt irritated; had he been deliberately lured away by the Grey Ghost?

'Can I borrow Caesar again, Henry?'

'Why not? If you're thinking of riding south, a fast horse may save your life.'

The wrangler, smiling, rolled a cigarette while Savage slapped his saddle on and headed for town.

There was no hurry now, and Caesar seemed to sense his mood and conserved his strength. When Savage reached Eden he hitched outside the Shamrock. Townsmen watched him, smiling openly; the news had spread and there'd be no trouble.

One Texan drawled: 'You going to arrest El Lobo? The only greaser to do us a favour!' He chuckled as if that were the joke of the year.

Maybe, Savage thought, and pushed into the saloon. Mike beamed from behind the bar and offered:

'Will you take a drink with me? There's no need

for bad feeling now.'

'Thanks, but I'm not much of a drinking man. Is Paloma around?'

Mike's hand hovered over a bottle.

'You're too late. As soon as she heard, she packed and was away across the border.'

'Was she now?'

Savage left the saloon and walked to the livery. The marshal was shoeing a horse while its rider watched and Savage waited until he'd finished.

Dutton wiped black and sweaty hands on what looked like his wife's old curtains, pocketed the money, and nodded.

Savage said: 'News travels fast. You've heard Channing was killed?'

'That's the way of news in Texas – it travels faster and further than anywhere else. The XL is out of my jurisdiction, so I'm not overly interested. You leaving us?'

'Going south.'

'That so?' Dutton scratched his head. 'Waal, let me tell you, son, across the border is El Lobo's home ground, and that gives him an advantage. Can't say I envy you, if you're serious.'

'I'm serious. Paloma's already left, I hear.'

'Paloma interests you? Take care how you handle that one. She's not what I call a homebody.'

Savage remembered how the dancer had excited him, and decided he had another reason to track her down.

The marshal said: ' 'Luck,' and offered his

hand. Savage gripped it, and left.

He was moving Caesar to a hitching post outside the emporium, ready to stock up for his trip when an accented voice hailed him.

'Mr Savage, I hope you'll join me in a last meal.'

It was the dude, standing on the steps of the hotel. Savage paused, considering; decided it was a good idea and said so.

'They've got onions today,' James Lacey enthused, 'and I've a fancy for steak and onions. I suppose you'll be leaving us soon.'

They walked into the dining-room and Lacey ordered as they sat down.

'I'm going south,' Savage said.

Lacey expressed surprise.

'Surely not? I've heard that even the Mexican police are wary of El Lobo, and you'll be alone.'

'Why is everyone so sure El Lobo killed Channing? Is a knife his usual weapon?'

Lacey considered this amusing.

'I'm sure I don't know. It's an assumption Texans make and I don't know why. Do you doubt it?'

'A knife is a woman's weapon, and Paloma left town right after.'

The dude's innocent blue eyes opened wide.

'Surely you can't suspect her? I'm almost certain she was performing till late last night.'

Conversation stopped as their meals arrived and they both concentrated. Over coffee, Lacey asked:

'How is Mrs Channing taking his death?'

'She seems remarkably calm.'

'I really must hire a buggy and drive out. See if she needs help – there must be something I can do.'

Savage drank a second cup and pushed back his chair.

'Thanks, but I want to be in Mexico before dark.'

'Good luck, then.'

Savage crossed the dusty street to the emporium and told the storekeeper what he wanted: shells for his shotgun, coffee, matches, jerky, and grain for Caesar. He had no idea what to expect below the Rio Grande.

As he collected his purchases, he noticed a display of knives: some large, some small, some almost a duplicate of the one that had killed Mark Channing.

'Mexican?' he asked.

The pot-bellied storekeeper squinted at him. 'Yep. In my opinion, their craftsmen turn out some fine blades.'

Savage hefted one of the bigger ones, and decided he preferred his Bowie.

'Sell many?' he asked casually.

The storekeeper shrugged.

'Unfortunately, not many. Texans are preju- diced, and usually prefer their own steel.'

Savage nodded and loaded up. He rode out of town, down the river bank and Caesar entered the water without hesitation. The current caught them and swept them towards the far shore.

CHAPTER 5

SOUTH OF THE BORDER

Nuevo Eden was not quite a double of the town Savage had left. As he rode along a wide and dusty street lined with shacks and stores, he saw more dogs and barefoot kids. The buildings were mostly of adobe bleached a pale shade of grey, and the talk he overheard was conducted mainly in Spanish.

For the first time, an element of doubt crept into his mind. He hadn't considered the difference in language when he set out; he'd met Mexicans before and they usually spoke a kind of English well enough to make themselves understood. And this, after all, was a border town; but, beyond that. . . ?

Evening light was fading when he hitched

outside the largest cantina, a two-storey building, dismounted and pushed between the batwings into a shady interior. The air felt pleasantly cool and his throat was dry. There was a large mirror behind the bar and an assortment of bottles. A few North Americans sat around the place but he chose not to join them.

He walked up to the bar and asked:

'Coffee?'

'Sure thing,' said the swarthy man behind the counter. 'Stabling at the back. Take a seat at a table and the girl will bring your drink.'

Savage went outside, led Caesar around the building and gave instructions to a stable-hand. Then he returned to the cantina and chose a table where he could put his back against a wall.

A man was lighting the oil-lamps and differently coloured bottles glittered. He sniffed the air; someone was smoking a cheap cigar, but nobody took more than a mild interest in him.

A girl came from a back room with a jug of coffee and a large cup; she was maybe fourteen, he thought, with lively eyes and a thin dress that was too small for her.

'Teresa!'

She swerved as a customer made a grab for her. She stuck out her tongue and rattled off rapid Spanish that had other men laughing.

She brought the coffee to Savage's table.

'Anything else, *Yanqui*?' She struck a provocative pose that made him smile.

'Maybe your big sister.'

'Is that why you've followed me?'

Savage had heard that voice before, cool, challenging, and looked up. Paloma was coming down the stairs from rooms above the bar. She appeared relaxed and confident as she crossed the floor towards him.

She wore a tight-fitting gown and he found himself stirred again by this exciting woman.

'Share a coffee with me?' he asked.

'Why not?' She dropped into the chair beside him. 'Now that Channing is dead, there's no reason we can't be friends.'

The man behind the bar brought her another cup.

'Thanks, Carlos.'

Teresa snorted. 'If it's like that, goodbye, *gringo*. I don't fancy her leavings.'

'I've told you, sister, you're too young for the big men. And this one chased the Grey Ghost.'

'That so?' Teresa regarded Savage with interest. 'I heard something about that. I'd like to see this wonder horse.'

Paloma smiled sweetly. 'She fancies herself an expert on horseflesh.'

'While you fancy yourself an expert on man flesh!' Teresa retorted, and flounced away.

Savage poured more coffee, amused.

'Are you two really sisters?'

'Really . . . She seems to have appointed herself my guardian.' Paloma looked him over. 'And you,

47

do you think yourself man enough to satisfy me?'

'I'll demonstrate when you're in the mood but first, what do you know about Channing's murder? Was the killer El Lobo?'

'Murder? He deserved what he got!' Her face twitched with suppressed laughter. 'And now you are looking for El Lobo? A joke, *sí*?'

'No joke,' he said said, and pushed back his chair. 'But that can wait, and I can't.'

Paloma rose in one graceful movement and led the way upstairs. She pushed open the first door at the top and Savage crowded in behind her. He smelt perfume and sweat, excitement building.

He kicked the door shut as she unfastened a button to let her gown slide below her shoulders. Pointed breasts dug into him as he grabbed her. His breath quickened as she rubbed her belly against him and tugged him towards the bed.

They fell together on to the bed, Savage trying to free his belt and get his pants down while she lifted her skirt. His need was so urgent that after the first explosion he collapsed.

And found he was a prisoner. He hadn't realized before that a professional dancer had strongly developed muscles until her thighs clamped like a vice. She whispered:

'Again, and slowly this time.'

It seemed a long while before she relaxed her grip and let him fall back, exhausted. It was pleasant just to lie there, studying the pattern made by cracks in the ceiling.

He remembered there were questions he wanted answers to.

'Channing's death – was El Lobo responsible?'

She pouted. 'That joke again?' She reached for a bottle on the bedside table, pulled the cork and drank, then passed it to him.

'What's this?'

'Tequila. When in Mexico, this is what you drink.'

Savage sniffed at the open neck of the bottle, and handed it back.

'Thanks, but I'm not really a drinking man. Now, about the Wolf . . .'

She gave an expressive sigh.

'You must be a madman, so why not ask him yourself?'

'You can direct me to him?'

'I can arrange for you to meet – if you're sure that's what you want. Paloma can arrange anything. Think carefully, lover, because not many seek out El Lobo and live.'

'Arrange it,' Savage said, and closed his eyes.

Savage sat at ease in a chair in the shade of the cantina. He rested his shotgun across his knees and sipped from a glass in his hand. No one bothered him. Word seemed to have got around that he was under Paloma's protection, so he waited patiently for her to set up the meeting.

He noticed the locals disappearing about the same time as he heard a parade of riders come into town. They came slowly and by the time their leader reached the cantina the street was deserted.

El Lobo? Savage frowned. He saw that the riders wore dust-coated uniforms; two mounted men rode behind their leader, followed by three men on foot, each holding a dog on a leash.

Savage sharpened up. Police? He waited, watching.

The man in front, on as fine a roan horse as Savage had seen, reined back and stared down at him with a supercilious expression. He was a Mexican and dapper with a slimline moustache and so much gold braid he might have been part of a circus.

He spoke in correct, but stilted English.

'I am Captain Rodrigo, sometimes known as "Rodrigo of the Rurales".'

He paused, and Savage nodded.

'You are the *gringo* hunting El Lobo?'

'Word surely gets around.' Savage eyed the dogs and shifted his grip on the shotgun. 'But, yes, I'd like to question your bandit.'

The dogs strained at their leashes; each leash was made of iron links and their collars were thick leather. Their handlers needed to exert some strength to hold them back.

The animals' ribs showed, as if starved, their heads were pointing hungrily at him; he saw mouths filled with sharp teeth.

'Hunting dogs?' he asked.

The captain smirked.

'In a way, *señor*. They have been trained to kill when released. Pardon me, I must get a drink. Then we shall talk.'

Rodrigo stepped down from his horse and Savage saw he had short legs, too short for his average-sized body, giving him the appearance of a dwarf. Obviously, disease or an accident had stunted his growth. He waddled into the cantina.

Savage watched the dogs watching him. They were large with shaggy triangular heads and he could smell them. They made a low growling sound that filled the air with menace.

Captain Rodrigo returned with an opened bottle. He took the chair next to Savage and drank till, with a huge sigh, he relaxed.

'That is better. Now, tell me, please, why you wish to question El Lobo.'

'He is suspected of killing a man north of the border.'

'One only?' Rodrigo lifted an eyebrow. 'Here he has killed many . . .'

One of the dogs lunged forward and the handler clubbed it into submission. Rodrigo snapped something in Spanish, smiled at Savage and continued:

'So how will you find him when I, who have chased him for so long, cannot? He can be as elusive as a shadow.'

'A mutual friend is arranging a meeting.'

'A friend?'

Savage kept silent; he was not sure he trusted this policeman.

Rodrigo lowered his voice. 'You wish for the reward, perhaps?'

'Reward?' Savage was startled.

'*Sí*, there is a useful sum for the head of El Lobo. You did not know? Perhaps you could use some help?'

'Perhaps,' Savage said cautiously.

'You are ignorant of the country and our language. I, on the other hand, speak English – that puts me one up, *sí*? We would share the reward. You meet the bandit chief while we follow you at a distance. Perhaps between us we can trap this one who has the ability to be in two places at once.'

'That must be quite a trick.'

'You laugh, but you had best take me seriously, *señor*. The reward is dead or alive!'

Savage considered his position, and decided some back-up could prove useful.

'Why not?' he said lightly. 'I'm not here for the reward.'

'Excellent – if true. We have a pact. Let me know when you leave, and I shall follow.'

Captain Rodrigo emptied his bottle and tossed it aside. He climbed on to his roan and moved off, men and dogs following.

Savage sat on the edge of the bed in Paloma's room, pulling his boots on. She lay there, naked,

52

watching him, black hair spread out.

'Such a stupid thing to do – it is a shame. Can you truly believe El Lobo will allow you to return?'

'I don't intend to allow him any say in the matter.'

She made a noise expressing contempt.

'You are a fool, and Rodrigo is a pig. Do not trust that one.'

Savage said; 'I'm not in the habit of trusting anyone. Have you the directions I need?'

'*Sí*. Teresa will take you to the foot of a mountain path, riding a mule. She will point out the way and exchange mounts. A mule is better for that kind of path, and she will ride your horse back – she's looking forward to that. Just sit on the mule and it will get you to the top.' She shrugged. 'After that, El Lobo decides.'

Savage finished dressing, adjusted his Bowie and picked up his shotgun. He headed for the door.

'Such a pity.' She sounded almost tearful. 'We made the good loving, *sí*?'

'I'll be back,' Savage assured her. He went out and down the stairs.

CHAPTER 6

FIVE GOLD COINS

Although the ground was rising steadily towards the mountains, Savage had to keep Caesar on a tight rein: the chestnut wanted to run. Teresa sat on a mule determined to take life at its own pace.

The young Mexican had her gaze fixed on Caesar and obviously approved of the way he moved.

'*Sí*, a horse that wants to race,' she murmured. 'I can see he will run well, so I personally will take care of him when you fail to return.'

Her smile was sly, and he wondered what she knew that he didn't. She resembled Paloma only in one way: where Paloma put dancing first, she put horses.

'My sister should not waste her talents on men,' she said severely. 'She is a dancer.' Her English wasn't bad, but not yet as good as Paloma's.

'How about giving me my first lesson in Spanish?' Savage suggested.

'You are going to walk into El Lobo's den and you want lessons in Spanish?' Teresa rolled her eyes upwards. 'You are even stupider than I suspected! What you need is a lesson on how to get back to Yanqui-land quickly. El Lobo will make a meal of you and spit out the bones.'

She gestured at their back trail, where Rodrigo and his men were following.

'And if you are relying on those, write your will now. They will kill you almost as soon as El Lobo!' She laughed. 'But this talk of death is not good, so I'll tell you a tale of a Mexican hero – a *vaquero* – one of those who taught your cowboys to rope the longhorns.

'Listen, his horse fell in front of a stampeding herd so he faced the horns and drew his revolver. He waited till the leader was almost on him, then shot it dead. As it fell at his feet, the herd split in two, like the waters parting in the Bible, and went around him. We have them too, you see.'

Savage smiled. 'You mean tall stories?'

She poked out her tongue at him. Ahead of them the grass became sparse and the hill track rose sharply.

'Here,' she said, and slid from the saddle.

The mule started to graze as Savage dismounted and handed her Caesar's reins. He climbed on the mule, shotgun in hand.

'You will find El Lobo waiting for you at the top,'

she said, unsmiling, and vaulted on to the chestnut. '*Adios, gringo.*' She dug her toes into the horse's sides and galloped away.

Obviously she had no doubt of the outcome as Savage started up to meet the bandit chief, urging the reluctant mule into motion.

He used the slack of the reins as a whip and kicked its flanks. The animal proceeded slowly and he sat like a statue in the saddle.

The path was easy at first, then the grass ended and the way got steeper. There was rock under the mule's hoofs, and loose stones; the animal slowed even more, taking one step at a time.

Savage sat very still as the path narrowed and the drop on one side stretched away. Despite the heat of the sun he felt a chill.

The silence was broken only by a chirping of insects. The path zigzagged upwards and he saw, below, Rodrigo with his men start to follow him. Teresa on Caesar was almost out of sight.

He eventually reached the summit, which was more or less flat with a few tufts of coarse grass. The mule began to graze as soon as he slid from the saddle and stretched his legs.

He looked about and saw no one. The track ended at a ravine with a long drop, too wide for man or horse to jump. A single tree, stripped of its branches, lay horizontally across the gulf: a bridge to the far side, where there were boulders big enough to hide an army.

As he studied the rocks, a man walked out from

concealment, a big Mexican with a luxuriant moustache.

He wore a sombrero and had a bandoleer stuffed with cartridges across his chest. He carried a rifle.

'Hi, *gringo*,' he said cheerfully. 'I am called El Lobo. If you still want to talk, cross over!'

Savage looked at the tree-trunk spanning the gulf and suddenly it seemed narrower, barely the width of his boot. For many, it would have been a challenge. . . .

He remembered his early days as an orphan and and thief in New York. He'd been coming out of Mossy's pawnshop after exchanging a gold watch and chain for a few dollars when he was spotted by one of the gangs. Their leader, known as 'the Fish' because his name was Haddock, and his followers were all older and bigger than he was.

'Share it out,' the Fish commanded, holding out a large and grubby hand.

'Or we'll mob yuh,' added one of his lieutenants.

Savage had one advantage; he was small and fast on his feet. Like an eel, he slipped past the Fish and ran with the gang at his heels.

The time was late evening and the light was fading as he made for the area of dockland he knew best. There was a nest of derelict buildings, partly knocked down before rebuilding started. Empty warehouses loomed, and shuttered offices reared up in gloomy silence, some jutting out over dark oily water as it sloshed against the jetties.

There was a warren of alleyways, niches and shadows. He noticed a rusty ladder going up to a grey sky, and climbed. The Fish was big, with a belly, and Savage could easily outdistance him on a ladder. Most of the building's walls had gone and only iron girders stood like a giant frame; part of the roof sagged, about to collapse. He reached the top of the ladder and paused for breath.

Below him, some of the gang were cursing as they started up after him. He looked around for an escape route and there was just a single horizontal girder reaching out over space, its free end not attached to anything. But, under him, at the far end of the girder, he saw the roof of another building.

Before the Fish could reach him, Savage walked the twelve-inch girder. Height didn't worry him the way it did some people, and he had good balance. He reached the far end and looked back.

The Fish stood at the top of the ladder scowling at him. Savage held out his money and taunted:

'Come and get it!'

The Fish didn't move. He swore bitterly, but he didn't have the nerve to follow.

Savage jumped into space, landed sprawling on the roof below and made his escape. . . .

Savage looked at the tree trunk and kept a straight face. Shotgun in hand, he stepped on to the makeshift bridge and tested his footing. The tree trembled beneath his weight, shifting slightly; fortunately, the wood was dry. He took a deep breath and began walking.

He knew that under him was a long drop to certain death, but he kept his gaze on El Lobo's face, watching his expression change from amused contempt to frowning admiration. When he reached the centre of the bridge he felt the trunk move subtly but kept walking.

The Mexican removed his sombrero and bowed mockingly.

'Well done, *señor*. You are the first of those who hunt me to make the crossing.'

Savage stepped on to firm ground and El Lobo bent over and grasped the end of the tree trunk. He heaved once and it dropped away. Savage was isolated, with no way back and no chance of help from the Rurales.

He could have shot the bandit chief, but had no doubt he was covered by guns behind the rocks around him.

El Lobo resettled his sombrero to shade his eyes. 'I have a feeling we shall get on better without an interruption from "Rodrigo of the Rurales".' He made the title sound like a clown's act from a circus. 'This way, if you please.'

Savage followed because there was nothing else he could do.

The path sloped down to a hollow where horses grazed and men lazed about a camp-fire, drinking and smoking. One bandit tended a large pot suspended above the fire; there was an appetizing smell.

Savage noted that not all the bandits were Mexican, and guessed that the Anglos were outlaws who had been chased south. A few were wild-looking Indians.

The cook passed him a tin filled with stew and a spoon. It contained chilli so hot he gasped for air and a grinning man passed him a skin bag to wash his mouth out. The bag held a red wine so crude he shuddered.

El Lobo seemed amused.

'You are not used to the real chilli, the way we like it south of the Bravo.'

A tall thin man, his right ear missing, spoke rapidly in Spanish. El Lobo waved his hand nonchalantly. 'Relax, Gomez. Señor Savage is our guest.'

To Savage he explained: 'Gomez is my lieutenant, my right hand, and suspects all Yanquis.'

The cook passed Savage a mug of coffee, and El Lobo lit a cheroot.

'I believe you have questions.'

Savage nodded. 'A lot of people across the river believe you killed the rancher, Mark Channing.'

El Lobo's expression turned sour.

'Of course I did – he was a double-crossing rat! Surely you cannot object because I responded to the blackest treachery? Such an act cannot be forgiven.'

Savage almost choked on his coffee.

60

'You knew him?'

'Knew him? Let me tell you about Señor Channing—'

Gomez interrupted again, and El Lobo waved him away. Impatiently, he said:

'Gomez seems to think you're some kind of lawman.'

'The unofficial kind,' Savage admitted.

El Lobo smiled. 'And we all know what that means, *sí*? So, about Channing. I recruited him to play a second 'El Lobo' to fool the local police with my ability to be in two places at once – we make the raid while I am obviously elsewhere, you understand?'

Savage nodded and, for the first time noticed that the bandit's build was similar to that of Channing.

A look of contempt creased the Mexican's swarthy face.

'But our success was not enough for that one – he was greedy, and so must rob a church!' El Lobo crossed himself. 'He stole silver accumulated across centuries and used it to buy a ranch – and it is I who get the blame and am hunted by Rurales for nothing at all! These same Rurales who are little more than tax-collectors.

'They call us bandits, but what are they? They tax the peasants, who have little, so the wealthy politicos can live without the need to sweat. They are the real bandits in our poor country, is that not so?'

'*Sí*,' murmured Savage.

There was a moment's silence. El Lobo seemed to be contemplating what more he might do to Mark Channing were he still alive. Then he sighed.

'So, you see, a traitor, a sinner who—'

'And that's why you stuck a knife in his back?'

El Lobo gave a roar like a mountain lion.

'Who says this? It is a lie – never have I done such a thing. I am afraid to face no man!'

'I saw the body,' Savage said. 'He's dead enough to suit even you, knifed in the back with a Mexican blade.'

'Then El Lobo did not kill him,' the bandit chief said firmly.

'Someone did.'

'Not me, *señor*.' El Lobo lit a fresh cheroot from the butt of the old one. 'I wonder, but it no longer matters. He is dead. Meanwhile you, I think were not always a lawman?'

'He sure ain"t no Texan,' one of the Anglos put in.

'I'm from New York,' Savage said. 'I worked the dockside, and the cops never caught me.'

El Lobo beamed. 'I knew it.' He looked meaningfully at the Bowie sheathed at his waist. 'Is that your choice of weapon? To convince me you must prove yourself as a fighter.'

One of the Mexicans snorted his disgust.

'A knife fighter? Let me cut the kid a little!'

El Lobo frowned. 'Sometimes, Manuel, your tongue forgets itself. Be silent.'

Savage studied Manuel; thickset, with the beginning of a belly. He wouldn't be especially fast.

'I'll fight him if you want,' he said.

A cheer went up. To the bandits, a fight was entertainment, and they gathered around. El Lobo's frown lifted.

'That is well said.'

Savage handed his shotgun to the chief bandit and loosened his Bowie in its sheath. Manuel faced him, grinning; obviously he considered the Yanqui so much meat to be sliced.

'Quiet,' El Lobo said, and all Savage could hear was quickened breathing. He studied the ground and tested his footing.

Manuel posed like a matador before a bull. El Lobo announced:

'When I say "fight", you begin. When I call "enough", you finish.'

Manuel crouched, knife held low, ready to bring up it up in a disembowelling movement. The blade was Spanish, long and slender with an ornamented handle.

'Fight,' said El Lobo, and Manuel advanced, confident of victory.

Savage drew his Bowie in one swift eye-defeating movement and reversed his grip so that he held the blade in his fingers. He judged the distance and made his throw. The knife somersaulted once and the heavy hilt struck Manuel's temple.

He gave a small cry, his knees buckled and his knife dropped to the ground.

Savage walked forward and pushed the Mexican off-balance. He picked up both knives, sheathed his own and handed Manuel's to El Lobo, hilt first.

Gomez snarled something in Spanish, but El Lobo shook his head.

'He says you took Manuel by surprise – but he should not have been taken by surprise.'

El Lobo returned his shotgun, and Savage checked the load.

Manuel sat up, holding his head. He was not fully aware when El Lobo leaned forward and said:

'Keep very still, Manuel.'

The bandit froze as El Lobo put the point of the knife to his throat and drew its lightly across, using just enough pressure to break the skin so it leaked blood.

'That is to remind you, Manuel, that the gringo spared your life. But I shall not if you fail again. Do I make myself clear?'

Manuel nodded dumbly, and El Lobo tossed the blade at his feet. For a moment, the bandit hesitated, then picked it up.

El Lobo took a last puff on his cheroot, crushed it underfoot and turned to Savage.

'You will do one job for me, *sí*? Then you are a member of my wolf-pack. We love to fight, we take our women where we find them, we share our bottles. That is good, *sí*? A fine life!'

Savage said, 'I like to get paid.'

El Lobo sighed. 'You Yanquis are all the same – you put money first all the time. What a way to live!

64

But there is still Rodrigo, a nothing, a pest. Shall we say one hundred American dollars?'

Savage felt he was missing something until El Lobo expanded.

'Is it a deal? For one hundred you will rid me of this clown.'

It seemed wise to agree, and the Mexican produced five gold coins, each worth ten dollars.

'Half now – I shall pay the rest after I have visited the bank at Nuevo Eden. This is information the captain will want, so you will be able to get close to him. And now, a horse for our guest.'

One of the Anglos slung a saddle on to the back of a grazing horse and led it to him.

El Lobo pointed to a downward trail. '*Adios, amigo,* and good luck.'

The sun was sinking as Savage rode away. Behind him, Gomez scratched at the scar where his ear had been and grumbled:

'Foolishness. Alive, that one can only bring us trouble!'

CHAPTER 7

THE DOG TRAINER

Savage slept rough in the foothills, pondering the death of Mark Channing. If El Lobo was not the killer. . . ? Of course, the Mexican might be lying, but Savage was inclined to believe him.

He rose early and drank from a stream. By the time he reached Nuevo Eden sunlight dazzled and dogs lay panting in the shade. The town seemed unchanged in his absence. Only the youngest children appeared to have any energy as they chased a rag ball in the dusty street.

One small boy approached eagerly, holding out a grubby hand. '*Señor, señor, El Capitan . . .*'

He tried to reach the reins to lead him, but failed. Savage tossed him a coin and followed him to a long single-storey building. Outside, the Rurales sat smoking and drinking; he saw only two dog-handlers with their dogs crouched beside a bowl filled with water.

Both dogs lifted their heads to watch him with hungry interest. Savage hitched his borrowed horse and walked inside; the place was a billiard-hall.

Only one table was in use, by Captain Rodrigo. The third handler and his fearsome animal kept a few locals pinned against the far end of the room while the officer practised different strokes.

Rodrigo leaned across the table, cue moving smoothly. After pocketing a ball, he waddled around the table on his short legs to replace it on the cloth.

To Savage he appeared to be an expert, leaving the cue-ball where he could reach it, playing a cannon off the cushion. He wondered if he were being kept waiting deliberately; then the captain straightened, holding his cue as if it were a weapon.

'So, you have not arrested El Lobo?' He looked suspicious and sounded frustrated.

'That's true, but I did get to talk to him, and came away with a piece of news you'll want to hear.'

Rodrigo turned to the dog-handler.

'Did you hear that, Ferdi? A piece of news he brings me, when what I want is the head of El Lobo!'

Savage glanced at the dog-handler, a squat figure whose forearms rivalled those of Eden's blacksmith. His skin was the colour of copper and his features part-Indian.

Ferdi grunted a monosyllable while his dog strained at the chain; the animal had a mouthful of teeth that looked as if they'd been filed to points. Ferdi's other hand casually flicked a whip.

'Ferdi trains my dogs,' Rodrigo said. 'They obey him, and he obeys me.'

Savage nodded politely.

'Prisoners confess their crimes promptly when faced by one of Ferdi's dogs. If I threaten to turn one loose they tell me what I want to know.'

'More likely what they think you want to hear.' Savage murmured under his breath.

'So what news do you bring me? And why should I believe you?'

'El Lobo is planning to raid the bank here.' Savage didn't mention the money the bandit had given him. 'He boasted quite openly about this.'

Rodrigo made a sour face.

'That's it? You have no idea which day? We must wait around for El Lobo to arrive in his own time?'

'That's it,' Savage confirmed.

Rodrigo paced up and down, smacking the cue into the palm of his hand.

'I suppose we must remain in Nuevo Eden and set a watch on the bank. All right, we'll do that – and you will watch with us.'

He looked sharply, distrustfully at Savage.

'Ferdi, tell this gringo how you train your dogs.'

The handler smirked. '*Sí, sí, mi capitan.*' He glanced at Savage. 'It is simple. I starve them. When they are truly hungry, we allow a prisoner to

68

escape for them to hunt.'

Rodrigo interrupted. 'Mexican prisons are not the luxury cells yours are, Yanqui. A prisoner always takes any chance to escape.'

'If they bring him down,' Ferdi continued, 'I let them feed, but not for long. Only long enough to satisfy the worst pangs of hunger – then I use my whip on them to show who's boss. A hungry dog hunts better.' He indicated the dog he was holding back. 'Drum is fully trained and seems to have an appetite for human flesh.'

Savage looked at Drum, crouched to spring, and remembered that he, too, had not yet had breakfast.

'I'll be around,' he said. 'I've some unfinished business with Paloma.'

Gomez muttered again, 'I don't like it. The Yanqui means trouble.'

El Lobo stroked his moustache. 'Trouble? Since when have we not had trouble? The gringo may yet prove useful.'

He wasn't worried what an unofficial lawman from above the Bravo might do. What disturbed him was the idea that anyone should believe him capable of sneaking behind an enemy to stab him in the back. Such an idea affronted his pride.

He was a man, and afraid of no one!

Always he attacked openly, by daylight, leading at the head of his men as a real leader must. He felt the need to do something spectacular to protect his reputation, something more than raid a small town bank.

He would change the target from Nuevo Eden to somewhere altogether grander; after all, he was El Lobo. This must be such a raid as to bring tears of despair to Rodrigo's eyes – and then he remembered San Pedro, where the captain had his headquarters. The bank there would have much money for the taking and it was close by the Rurales' district headquarters.

While Rodrigo waited in Nuevo Eden, he would strike terror into the hearts of those Rurales left in San Pedro. It would be, he imagined, like chasing headless chickens. What a surprise! It would be a raid that was talked about for months, perhaps years.

He laughed out loud and Gomez asked:

'What is it you find so amusing?'

El Lobo told him. Gomez rubbed his scar and said:

'It is a good.'

El Lobo clapped his hands and his men gathered around.

'Listen, because Gomez is pleased.' There were cheers when he described the easy pickings at the bank in San Pedro.

'So, let us get ready. I want every man on this raid, fully armed. You will need extra ammunition, a spare horse and double waterskins.

'Gomez, you will check every detail. I personally shall lead to make sure that Rodrigo curses the day he thought to pursue El Lobo and his pack of wolves!'

After a large breakfast, Savage walked to the cantina. Behind the counter, Carlos opened one eye, then closed it again. The place was almost empty in late morning and Paloma sat alone at a table drinking coffee and yawning. She wore an old dressing-gown, no make-up and regarded him with a baleful eye.

'Did you enjoy your little chat, Señor Savage?'

'Enjoy is not the word I'd choose but, yes, our talk was certainly interesting. First he said "yes", and then he said "no", so maybe it wasn't El Lobo at all. Which opens up the field. Can you think who else might slip a knife into a man's back? A man who, apparently, didn't trust anyone? Did you know that was how Channing died?'

She made a smile that reminded him of a cat.

'No, at first I didn't know – only that he was dead.' She sipped her coffee. 'Who else but a woman? Who else would he not fear? Someone close to him, maybe?'

'Maybe. I'm wondering about you.'

'I was dancing, *sí*?' She pouted. 'I'm sure any man in the Shamrock that night would say I was dancing.'

'I'm sure they would. Was your sister across the border that night?'

'Teresa? You'll have to ask her – she's a law unto herself.'

71

'I shall. I need to find out what she's done with my horse.'

'Of course! It was silly of me to think you might have been looking for me. Your horse . . . Try the stable at the back.' Paloma jerked a thumb in the direction of the rear door. 'I'll warn you, my little sister thinks of it as her horse now. She's always been horse-mad and now has big plans.'

Savage walked through a doorway into the yard. Across the yard he saw the stable door wide open. Inside, Teresa was grooming Caesar and talking to him in Spanish. The stallion stood waiting patiently, listening.

'Guess he's never had it so good,' Savage said.

The girl looked around, frowning.

'You're back!' There was dismay in her voice, but she recovered quickly. 'Listen, I intend to race this one. I'm sure we can deal.'

Savage shook his head.

'I only borrowed Caesar, and have to return him. Besides, I need to ask you: were you across the border the night Channing was killed?'

'What if I was? Although I didn't kill him, I would have if I'd had the chance! That's not important now. Just listen . . .'

She stroked the chestnut and her eyes pleaded with Savage.

'He's fast, faster even than . . .' Her voice fell away and suddenly she grinned, looking more like a child. 'You don't need to know that, Yanqui. Let me ride him and I – we – could make some money.

72

Perhaps a lot of money.'

'Maybe.' Savage thought about it; money was always useful. Rodrigo wanted him to help guard the bank and wasn't likely to let him slip away until the trap had been sprung, so . . .'

'Why not?' he said. 'We'll split any winnings fifty-fifty, *sí?*'

'*Sí.*'

CHAPTER 8

THE SIESTA RAID

It was a question of timing, El Lobo mused. San Pedro was a big and busy town, so he would strike when least expected. He had already decided there was no advantage to be gained by slowly infiltrating in twos and threes; not at midday.

Nobody worked during the noonday heat, so the men of the town would be indulging in a siesta; flat out in the shade, eyes closed, and possibly with a bottle. As would his own men given the chance.

Sweat trickled from his hatband and ran down his face but he refused to wipe it away; he had to set an example. He rode at the head of his men, watching the sun as they watched him. He was hot and sticky, his men and animals too, but only Gomez dared remark on it.

'Is it necessary to punish ourselves like this?'

El Lobo stuck one end of a cheroot in his mouth

and struck a match. He inhaled deeply before he spoke.

'It is necessary to take San Pedro by surprise. It is necessary to show the Rurales we do not hide behind the skirts of women. It is necessary to show Rodrigo that he cannot stop us doing what we please. That is what is necessary, *amigo*, and a little discomfort to achieve that is nothing, nothing at all.'

Gomez remained silent and some of the men looked sullen, but not one challenged him.

El Lobo enjoyed his cheroot as the trail wound down between farms towards the town. The sight recalled his youth to mind; he knew about small farms that produced only a subsistence level of living. They meant hard work, and the peons were easy-going: *things would be better tomorrow.* Always it was *mañana,* any excuse to put off making an effort.

El Lobo had found that extra energy. Women admired his energy and to retain their admiration he assumed the mantle of leadership of a small group of rebels. Their numbers had grown until they had become a thorn in the flanks of the Rurales and a friend to small farmers. Always there was a scattering of small coins to the peons to make sure the Rurales were misdirected.

He remembered the women, and thought he must be getting old. He was growing tired of being hunted. It was time to strike back, even if the gringo failed him.

When he reached the outskirts of the town, El Lobo put his horse to the trot and sat straight in the saddle. The others followed. This was how Captain Rodrigo returned from a hunt; and who else would so boldly enter San Pedro in daylight? Certainly not a gang of bandits with a price on their heads.

They passed adobe houses and shops and came to the central plaza. El Lobo remembered happier times when young beauties paraded with their duennas. There was no town band now.

A few stone buildings loomed; one was the bank, another the district headquarters of the Rurales.

El Lobo threw down the butt of his cheroot in a shower of sparks; this bank was notorious for the foreclosing of overdue mortgages on farms. It would be a pleasure to take money from such grasping hands.

The sun blazed down on an almost empty square; a few drinkers half-dozed at tables beneath striped awnings. Sleepy eyes registered a body of riders . . . seconds passed before the few observers quietly vanished.

El Lobo smiled. It seemed he wouldn't get a lot of opposition from the townsfolk even when their siesta ended. Harness jingled as men dismounted.

'Let the animals drink. Gomez, watch closely the offices of the Rurales. They may have a man on duty who is not asleep.'

El Lobo took three men with him, each carrying a canvas sack. The heavy doors of the bank stood open, but there was only one clerk behind the counter. He was mildly surprised to see customers at this time of day; then his eyes opened wide.

El Lobo jabbed his chest with the muzzle of his rifle.

'Silence! Attempt to give an alarm and you are a dead man. Fill these sacks with banknotes and coins – whatever you have to hand, and quickly. Wake up, now!'

The first bandit thrust a sack into the clerk's hands.

'*Sí, sí,*' the man mumbled, opening a drawer. With shaking fingers he began to stuff the sack with money.

'Faster!'

A second bandit passed him a sack when the first man walked out to his horse.

The manager stepped from a back room, holding a sheet of paper. He stopped suddenly as El Lobo waved the rifle in his direction.

'So far I have killed no one today. Do you wish to be the first?'

The manager gasped and dropped the sheet of paper as his hands shot into the air.

Gunfire echoed outside.

'Enough. Time to leave!'

The third bandit grabbed his sack and ran for the door. El Lobo strolled after him, contemptuous of both clerk and manager, but his pulse was beating quicker. . . .

*

Gomez watched the Rurales' office in the plaza and scratched at his missing ear. He felt uneasy. His horse moved restively.

It was going too well. One man already out of the bank with a sack of money. Only two more and . . .

A gunshot blasted the quiet and he twisted in the saddle to look across the plaza. Despite the heat, a lone man was coming towards them at a run, a big revolver in his hand. An old Mexican, shooting wildly as he shouted: '*Viva Mexico!*' His bullets missed by yards, but the sound would wake the Rurales.

'It's only . . .' he started to say, when a single shot came from behind him and the old man collapsed in the dust.

Gomez turned to see 'Texas' Pete laughing. An Anglo; he might have known.

'There was no need for that,' he said, and crossed himself.

El Lobo followed the third man from the bank, demanding:

'What's happening?'

'Pete got gun-happy,' Gomez said angrily, 'and shot down old Ramon – a harmless old man reliving the war he fought against the Texans. He was in the army and took a head wound.'

One of the Indians began to shake, muttering:

'Bad, very bad medicine . . . to hurt one possessed by the gods! Very, very bad luck now!' He ended in a wail.

Bullets were already coming from the Rurales' office.

A few of his men were firing back; but too many just waited, spooked by the Indian. El Lobo knew they were a superstitious lot and cursed.

He swung into the saddle and turned his horse about.

'Go,' he shouted. 'Get out, fast!'

His shout broke the spell and his men followed, spurring their horses. A bullet passing between the ears of his mount encouraged the animal to a gallop. He leaned back, triggering his rifle as, only now, Rurales poured into the plaza with guns blazing.

A couple of them mounted horses and gave chase, but not for long. El Lobo's men were not noted for taking prisoners, and the captain was not present to urge them on.

El Lobo left town and took a hill track into the mountains. The Rurales were not going to press the chase hard but, at each farm, he scattered a few coins to ensure that any directions forced from the lips of the peons would be the wrong directions.

But the Rurales of San Pedro slowed once they reached the edge of town. They had been seen to try and that was enough. El Lobo had escaped again.

Outside the bank in Nuevo Eden, Savage took a chair in the shade and kept his head down.

He had been officially requested to stay with the captain's men, but now an excited crowd formed a screen around him. By standing, he calculated he would see whatever happened.

Rodrigo waddled from the bank on his short legs, stopped and frowned. He'd just finished warning the bank manager to expect a visit from El Lobo when, suddenly, the main throughway of the town resembled fiesta time.

'What is this, Ferdi? What's going on?'

His chief dog-handler hauled back on the leash that held Drum and grunted, 'Horse-race, *Capitan*. They are betting on a horse-race!'

'Now? With a notorious bank robber expected? Are they mad?'

His Rurales tried to look as if they were not enjoying themselves; some had already placed their money. So far five horses were entered for the race and Carlos, who seemed to be in charge of the event, asked, 'Are you entering, *Capitan*?'

Rodrigo snorted.

'I forbid this ridiculous race – at least, for the present time. We have serious business here.'

Someone in the crowd murmured: 'His horse is so slow, it's only for show.'

'Who said that?' Rodrigo demanded, but nobody answered.

Carlos said smoothly, 'It seems to me that, with a race taking place and most people on the street, even El Lobo might find it difficult to reach our bank.'

Rodrigo touched his slimline moustache and studied the crowded throughway; people lined both plankwalks.

'Perhaps there is wisdom in your words. *Sí*, I give permission for this race to take place.'

'And you will enter?' Carlos asked.

Rodrigo smiled.

'I shall enter, and win, of course. My roan will beat any other horse in a straight run.'

Maybe, Savage thought, remembering Caesar's chase after the Grey Ghost.

Again a voice from the crowd murmured:

'So put your money where your mouth is.'

The captain dug into a pocket of his uniform and brought out a purse. He opened it and took out one gold piece.

'This says I shall win!'

Carlos called for silence and announced:

'This race will follow our usual course, from the cottonwood just outside town to finish here at my cantina. For our visitors, that is a distance of one half-mile.'

That must be good for business, Savage thought, as he watched Teresa walk their horse along the road to the other end of town. The girl had the stallion well in hand; she was small and light and that gave her an advantage.

Carlos proclaimed, 'Prize money will be ten per cent of all bets.'

The crowd jostled and chattered in good humour, passing bottles and calling wagers and the Rurales seemed as excited as anyone.

Savage glanced towards the bank; its doors were closed and a bunch of kids stood on the steps to see over the heads of the crowd. If El Lobo showed up, the situation could be amusing.

He heard a distant gunshot signalling the start of the race and returned his attention to the empty street. Silence spread through the crowd as they craned forward to stare down the length of the course. A cloud of dust swirled upwards, then the heads of the leading horses showed. There was a burst of cheering.

'Teresa! Teresa's in front!'

'And *El Capitan*!" Mock groans came from some of the young.

Savage stood on his chair to see better. Those two were certainly in the lead, but closely followed by hard-riding horsemen flogging their mounts with quirts.

Caesar's ears were flat, his tail straight out behind. The young Mexican girl was lying along his neck, urging him on. Her attitude, low and close to the horse's back struck a chord in his memory.

He recalled another rider he'd glimpsed by starlight north of the border. Or was it possible this was the same rider? He decided it was, and that Teresa had questions to answer.

Rodrigo was sitting erect in his saddle as though leading a cavalry charge. Other riders galloped behind screaming at their mounts. There were wild yells from the crowd supporting whichever horse they'd backed. Teresa steered a straight course down the centre of the street. All the horses were going flat out, with Caesar and Rodrigo's roan neck and neck.

When the cantina came in sight, Teresa kicked Caesar and he shot ahead like a bullet from a gun. His stride lengthened as he lunged forward, taking the captain by surprise and streaking past the finishing line to be a clear winner.

A popular winner, to judge by the shouts of the spectators and those collecting their bets.

Savage watched Caesar slow down. His ugly head wrinkled in a ferocious grin and Savage had no doubt the stallion was pleased with himself.

From an upstairs window, Paloma called congratulations to her sister.

Teresa reined to a halt, smiling broadly.

'I knew, it – I knew Caesar could win for me!'

Savage started as a voice whispered in his ear:

'Watch Rodrigo – he doesn't like to lose.'

Savage nodded, and edged through the crowd. The captain's face as he dismounted was a mask of fury. He strode towards the girl who'd beaten all the men, and Ferdi with his dog followed.

CHAPTER 9

THE WHIP HAND

Captain Rodrigo trembled with rage. Words exploded from his lips. 'Cheat . . . you cheated me . . . it was my race all the way! Nobody cheats Rodrigo of the Rurales, nobody!'

Teresa, startled, began to move away. Ferdi's whip snaked out and curled around her wrist. One jerk of the lash and she stumbled towards the captain, who seized her and shook her violently.

'Admit it – you cheated me, and I am the winner!'

Teresa lifted her chin and stared him down.

'Caesar won the race. The fastest horse won.'

Rodrigo ground his teeth and turned to his men. 'Hold her.' As Ferdi released his whip, two of the Rurales grabbed her arms.

Rodrigo reached out, grasped the top of her dress and ripped it down about her waist.

'Back, back,' he shouted, and his men pulled

her around till her back was towards him.

'I shall make an example of this creature,' he shouted. 'No one lies to me – she cheated. Use your whip, Ferdi.'

Ferdi grunted with pleasure, and his features indicated that this was a particular pleasure. He jerked on the leash, Drum snarled and the crowd melted away.

The lash rose, and descended like a striking snake. It cut once and blood flowed. Teresa cried out with the shock, then closed her lips tightly. Her back showed a red weal as Ferdi raised his whip to strike again.

'Skin her!' Rodrigo ordered.

The street was almost deserted now; even Carlos had retreated into his cantina.

Savage frowned. The girl was, in a way, his partner – though perhaps this was not the time to claim their winnings.

'Calm yourself, Captain,' he said. 'I have a better use for this little one.'

Ferdi couldn't wait. He struck again, and this time she flinched but remained silent. Only then did he look towards his master for instructions.

Rodrigo glanced knowingly at Savage.

'This slut? You want to buy her? You prefer young flesh, is that it, gringo?'

Savage fumbled in his pocket; one ten-dollar coin might not tempt the captain to put off his revenge. He offered three of the coins El Lobo had given him.

'So!' Rodrigo calmed slightly, and held out a hand. 'I can wait, *señor*. Use her hard, and when you've finished, pass her back to me.'

He tossed the coins in the air, and caught them. 'A drink for all,' he said to his men, and waddled into the cantina. Only Ferdi looked sour.

Savage led Caesar towards the stable and Teresa stumbled after him, trying to hold up her torn dress.

'I'll rub him down,' he said. 'You'd better find your sister and get those cuts treated.'

She nodded and vanished through a shadowed doorway.

El Lobo was in an expansive mood. He had a bottle of brandy in one hand and a lighted cheroot in the other. He considered he'd proved himself yet again, and relaxed after a large meal, laughing at the crude jokes his men told.

Almost everyone around the camp-fire in the hills was happy with the share-out, the best they'd had for a while. Even Gomez, usually serious, joined in a card-game as bottles passed from hand to hand; a small group huddled over thrown dice and a couple of men stretched out on the ground and were soon snoring.

Only the Indians, sitting apart, seemed sunk in gloom. The death of old Ramon had upset them and now they expected nothing but bad news as a result of Pete's killing. They were like children, El Lobo decided; he had to do their thinking for them. Nothing could touch them here.

Suddenly he inclined his head to one side, ears straining. A rattle of loose stones below indicated a horseman arriving.

The sentry called:

'One rider.' After a pause, he added, 'A man from Carlos.'

'Let him through.' El Lobo picked up his rifle and pushed off the safety. He hadn't lived so long by being careless. But he recognized the man; one of those who occasionally helped out in the cantina.

'A message from Paloma,' the man called, and seemed reluctant to move close when El Lobo held out his hand for it. As soon as the bandit chief took the folded sheet of paper, the messenger stepped back.

El Lobo unfolded the paper and read the words written there. At first, their meaning didn't sink in; then he couldn't believe what he read. Then his expression changed and the messenger backed even further away.

The hands of El Lobo closed to make fists and words choked in his throat.

'Is this true? Can it be possible that Rodrigo dared to lay a hand on Teresa? Speak up!'

'It is true . . .' The messenger looked miserable. 'He ordered his dog-handler to use a whip on her.'

El Lobo turned pale with barely suppressed fury. He hissed:

'He whipped her in public? And nobody stopped him?'

'The Anglo, the one you talked to, he paid the captain for her—'

'He what?' If El Lobo had been a bomb he would have exploded. Savage had not only failed to kill Rodrigo, but had given money to the captain. His money!

Gomez chucked his cards on the ground in disgust.

'I warned you. We should have killed the Yanqui when we had him.'

But the bandit chief was blind and deaf to everything except this insult. He glared about and his face was like that of a wolf with the killing lust on him.

'Sober up! We are riding to Nuevo Eden. Rodrigo has finally gone too far, and will answer to me. I'll nail his skin to the stable door!'

The Indians glanced at each other. The bad times had begun . . .

Gomez protested:

'Let us wait – we know the Rurales are still there. Let us first spy out the situation.'

If it had been anyone else, El Lobo would have accused him of cowardice, but there was no fear in his lieutenant; that had been burned out long ago. He was completely loyal and his hatred of Rurales was legendary. . . .

When they'd first met, he'd been riding back after a visit to Maria, taking a short cut through a canyon in the badlands.

He didn't know his name then; he saw only a young Mexican peon one step from an ugly death.

Gomez had been spread-eagled across thorny mesquite in the sun; a straw hat lay discarded at his bare feet and his eyes were closed. Dried blood masked one side of his face where the ear had been sliced away. He was in agony and at the end of his strength; and collapsed immediately he was cut free.

El Lobo dragged the unconscious man into the shade and dropped the straw hat over his head. He fed him water, then water and brandy and lifted him into the saddle of his own horse. He walked through the badlands until he made camp for the night.

After more brandy and hot food the peon recovered sufficiently to tell his story:

'My father's farm failed, so, because he couldn't pay his taxes, the Rurales beat him senseless. Stupidly, I lost my temper and went for them – of course I stood no chance and was soon knocked down. They arranged a slow death and left me as, perhaps, you should have. Of what use am I now?'

'I am El Lobo, and a man who attacks Rurales is a man I have a use for. You will live many years and kill many Rurales.'

Gomez made a smile and held out a hand. El Lobo gripped it.

Since that day, he had shown himself to be loyal, a fierce fighter and cunning. He was quickly promoted to be his chief lieutenant.

Now he advised caution, but such was El Lobo's rage that he refused to listen.

'We ride!'

Captain Rodrigo perched on a high stool at the bar; seated that way his stunted growth was not so obvious. The cantina was empty except for his own men and dogs, and Carlos behind the counter. Carlos was not happy, and sweat gathered on his swarthy face.

'Of course you will pay me my just winnings,' Rodrigo said. 'Everyone realizes the girl cheated and that I won the race.'

'Of course,' Carlos mumbled, and added desperately, 'I haven't collected all the money yet.'

'I shall wait here till you do collect it.'

Rodrigo liked the way the locals faded away after the race. Ferdi's dogs helped, of course. Their fear was necessary; it gave him the power to control them even though they outnumbered his men many times. Fear was what he relied on and used.

He drank alongside his men while he imagined the Anglo upstairs with the girl. He imagined her on her back.

He also wondered how good was Savage's information about the raid on the bank. He didn't particularly trust the gringo.

He put another of Savage's gold coins on the counter, and snapped:

'More tequila, Carlos.'

Distant guitar music sounded from a small

cantina further along the street. There was rarely music or dancing where the Rurales drank, and the favours of women had to be bought.

Ferdi's dog cocked its ears and turned to face the door.

Rodrigo frowned. From outside he heard a jingling of harness as a bunch of riders jogged into town. Was this El Lobo?

Through the window he could see that the riders wore uniform. They were his own men from San Pedro and should not be here at all. What was going on?

They stopped outside the cantina, dismounted and hitched, and their lieutenant came in.

He saluted.

'Sir, El Lobo's raiders robbed the bank in San Pedro. They got away with much money. We followed them part way, but . . .' He shrugged.

'But what?' Rodrigo felt red rage rising inside him. First, that girl; now this. Had El Lobo deliberately misinformed the gringo?

To raid the bank next to his own headquarters was sheer insolence; an insult to be wiped out in blood. He choked, washed out his mouth with tequila, spat, and threw the empty glass at Carlos.

'Feed and water your horses, Lieutenant. We are riding immediately. I shall not be satisfied until I have dealt with El Lobo and his bandits – and this time there will be no mercy!'

CHAPTER 10

AMBUSH

El Lobo rode at the head of his men and set a fast pace for Nuevo Eden. It was not a time for planning, but for action. He was hardly aware of his followers: Gomez, his right hand; Manuel, who liked to use a knife; Texas Pete who had killed old Ramon and spooked the Indians and left them fatalistic about the coming battle.

El Lobo rode in silence, as if wrapped in a cocoon that protected him from any outside influence. Where he was no bird sang; not even the heat of the sun reached him.

His face could have been carved from granite, yet inside he fumed like a volcano with lava rising to the surface. Rodrigo of the Rurales had dared to lay a hand on one of his and would pay with his life.

The face of Maria hovered before him like the

vision of a saint, and his expression softened for a moment. There had been other women, long-forgotten, but the memory of Maria still haunted him. He had been young and hot-blooded, passionate both as a rebel and a lover. Maria had been plump and willing, filled with laughter. 'My dumpling with the dimples' he'd called her.

It seemed a lifetime ago, and he wondered where all the years had gone.

Paloma, the first of his daughters, was born; then Teresa. And the decision, hard at the time but proved right over the years, had been for Maria to bring them up apart from him so they were not tainted by the name of Pascual, the rebel.

A doubly sensible move after he'd been named outlaw and a price put on his head. Leon Pascual vanished and El Lobo appeared.

He was proud of his daughters, cared fiercely and always supported them. He swore that Rodrigo would not touch either of them again.

El Lobo rode down from the hills with murder in his heart.

Rodrigo sat in the shade outside the billiard-hall while a small boy polished his riding-boots. The lieutenant had persuaded him to wait while his men ate a meal before setting out again, and now the captain was keeping them waiting.

The Rurales sat their horses, sweating in thick uniforms beneath a blazing sun. The lieutenant chafed at the delay but knew better than to say anything. Ferdi and the other two dog-handlers were keen for the hunt, the animals straining at their leashes. The locals watched from cover and prayed he'd leave.

Rodrigo gazed along the almost deserted street and saw a peon coming into town on a mule. The man appeared to be excited about something and was flogging the mule to move along faster.

The peon pulled up before him, sweat glistening on his whiskers, and gave a sloppy salute.

'Sir, I have this to report. El Lobo, with his men – many of them, are on their way here. This I have seen with my own eyes. They will arrive soon.'

Rodrigo smiled, and handed the man a gold piece.

'Well done!'

If the bandits were truly coming, he'd be ready for them; and now had the reinforcements his lieutenant had brought.

He tossed a small coin to the boot-boy, and stood up. It seemed to him that the good Lord was on his side, and the bandits were due a final reckoning. There was no need to go hunting in the heat; an ambush was a much better arrangement.

'Lieutenant, get your men off the street. Stable the horses and take cover. Use stores, cantinas, private rooms, anywhere you can see to fire from without being seen. The enemy is delivered to us. Shoot them down like the scum they are without mercy!'

Rodrigo would have danced a jig if his legs had been up to it.

Everything was working out satisfactorily, and El Lobo was riding into the trap that would end his career.

For a long moment the street seemed unnaturally quiet, the air still; even the flies were frozen in mid-air while the captain gloated and dreamed of collecting the reward.

A water-tap dripped, bringing him out of his reverie. There was no need to share this with the gringo. Savage could easily be shot, by accident, during the gun-battle.

Carlos started worrying the moment two Rurales walked into his cantina with guns in their hands and took up positions close to the batwings.

He had bottles on the shelves and a large mirror behind the counter and he didn't appreciate the casual attitude Rurales showed towards other people's property. Replacing damaged goods was an expense he could do without.

The few customers left quietly by the back door and he guessed they wouldn't return until this trouble was over. Carlos wanted to be agreeable to everyone, even Rurales. He was a businessman and liked to see money flowing in.

'Do you boys fancy a drink?' he asked with forced pleasantness.

One man hesitated. the other said:

'On the house?'

Carlos winced. '*Sí*, if you will be so kind as to put those guns away. Are you expecting bank-robbers?'

'We've heard that El Lobo will be visiting town.'

The Rurale paused, listening. No breeze stirred the silence and time seemed to have stopped.

Carlos crossed himself as he heard riders coming at a gallop.

Upstairs, Savage faced Teresa as she sat on the bed in her sister's room. She was dressed, but sitting rigidly upright; obviously her back still felt sore.

Paloma was angry with him.

'Why must you give her a bad time? Why don't you leave her alone?'

'Because I want answers to a few questions. Then she can do as she likes.'

'Stop worrying about me,' Teresa snapped at her big sister. 'I'll answer his stupid questions.'

Paloma's eyes glittered; she looked as if she might take a hairbrush to both of them.

'You told me you were north of the border the night Channing was murdered,' Savage said. 'Were you the one they called the Grey Ghost?'

Teresa sniffed.

'You are slow to catch on. Of course that was me, but I didn't kill him. Don't you believe me? I shot at him but didn't kill him. Whoever did shouldn't be called a murder. Channing deserved to die.' Her face was suddenly lit by a mischievous smile. 'Anyway, you couldn't catch me!'

'Do you know who killed him?'

'No, and I don't care. Is that all?'

Savage paused, aware that everyday street sounds had stopped; beyond the open window a stillness had settled over Nuevo Eden.

Then he heard a clatter of hoofs as a mass of riders entered town.

Paloma said: 'That'll be Father, now.'

Savage echoed: 'Father?'

Teresa laughed. 'El Lobo – you don't know much, do you? Paloma sent him a message.'

The idea took his breath away. At first, he was amused, and then worried. 'That may not have been such a good idea . . .'

A gunshot ripped the silence. He crossed to the window and looked out. The boardwalks were empty; the townsfolk had vanished; nor were there any Rurales to be seen.

He saw only mounted men with rifles, shotguns and machetes – El Lobo's men – bunched in the broad and dusty street below.

He heard El Lobo's voice raised in roar of rage.

'Come out and fight, Rodrigo – or are you nothing but a coward who beats on women?'

The captain ignored the challenge. He waited until the bandits started to dismount; then, from behind cover, he called:

'*Now!*'

A fusillade of gunfire swept the street from both sides. Caught in the open, men and horses went down. For what seemed like minutes there was a hell of confusion and screams from both men and animals. Savage's lips tightened.

El Lobo bellowed like a bull in the ring.

'Cowards! Take cover, *amigos*! Gomez, seek out Rodrigo and bring him to me. I have an itch to strip the flesh from his bones before he dies!'

Another barrage of gunfire filled the street with lead as the bandits scattered. Still the Rurales refused to show themselves and El Lobo's wolves smashed windows and doors to get at them.

The one called Texas Pete got tangled with the reins of his horse as a bullet spun him about; he fell and the horse stamped a hoof in his face. He tried to crawl away, shuddered and lay still.

Savage glimpsed hand to hand struggles with knives flashing and blood flowing. Revolvers cracked. A shotgun blasted and a man screeched his death agony.

Manuel's knife failed to save him when a club studded with nailheads opened him up.

Below, the window of the cantina shattered with a noise like a bomb going off as enraged bandits tried to get at their ambushers. It's getting too close, Savage thought.

El Lobo, on foot, was reloading his rifle when a stray bullet pierced the front of his throat and tore a hole in the back of his neck. He went down in a fountain of blood.

Gomez wailed: 'The wolf is down! Find the cowardly cur Rodrigo, and cut out his black heart!'

The Indian bandits began to silently steal away.

Beside Savage, Paloma turned pale, her body

rigid. Teresa produced a small revolver from some hidden place.

Rurales began to show themselves on the street and Savage heard a blood-freezing snarl. The handlers had unleashed their killer dogs.

On the street, Gomez hesitated a second too long. He shrieked as Drum hit him and drove him backwards to the ground. In a frenzy of blood-lust all three dogs were on him and Ferdi made no attempt to pull them off. The remaining bandits grabbed their mounts and scattered like straw in a gale.

As Paloma unsheathed a knife, Savage moved fast to block the doorway.

'No! You'd have no chance down there – the street is a death-trap.'

Paloma tried to push past him. 'It is our duty to avenge our father!'

'Maybe later, not right now.'

He grabbed Teresa as she tried to wriggle past him.

'We must,' she shouted. 'Let me go!'

Savage stood solidly, blocking their path.

'You can do nothing while those dogs are loose. Get ready to ride – I'm taking you both north before the Rurales start to look for you.'

As the shooting ebbed away, Rodrigo stepped from the billiard-hall, his gold braid flashing in the sunlight, a broad smile showing in his moment of triumph.

'I claim the head of El Lobo,' he declared in a

ringing voice. 'I claim the reward. It is mine alone. Why, I could get promotion – and a medal too. Imagine, Colonel Rodrigo of the Rurales!'

CHAPTER 11

MEXICAN FANDANGO

Savage heard Rodrigo's shout of triumph and knew they hadn't got long. He pushed the two girls away from him.

'Be ready to ride, and meet me at the stable. I'll saddle the horses.'

He moved quietly down the stairs, carrying his double-barrelled shotgun, pausing on the landing half-way to see who was in the cantina. Carlos, behind the bar, was pouring drinks for a couple of Rurales.

He continued down to the floor and walked towards the door, his face averted. He was almost to the batwings when they were pushed open from outside.

Rodrigo swaggered in, followed by Ferdi with

Drum. The other two dog-handlers were close behind, their animals leashed.

Savage backed towards the staircase, his mouth dry. Drum snarled. He lifted his shotgun.

Rodrigo came to life.

'The gringo – set the dogs on him!'

Savage continued to back away. They were large dogs, muscles tensed to spring, jaws open to show rows of teeth that would rip and tear.

He would have been scared if he'd had time, but Ferdi released Drum and the dog launched itself through the air. His finger instinctively tightened on a trigger.

The gun's blast ended with a howl of pain and a whimpering. One down and two to go.

He was still backing towards the stairs when a second dog gave a low growl. Its claws looked menacing and its eyes glowed like signals set at danger. Its jaw dripped saliva as if it couldn't wait to sink its teeth into human flesh.

As it left the ground in a giant leap, Savage triggered his second barrel, turned and sprang for the stairs. He took them three at a time. At the top he glanced back and saw the last dog feeding on the nearest carcass.

Ferdi had a gun in his hand and bullets slammed into the wall.

'Get him,' Rodrido screeched. 'A gold piece to the man who kills the gringo!'

No one appeared keen to earn the reward by following Savage upstairs. Rurales looked at each other and away from their captain. They hesitated until he bawled a direct order at them. Even then they advanced up the stairs with great caution. A man who dispatched killer dogs was someone to treat with respect. . . .

Upstairs, at the end of the passage, Paloma beckoned to Savage.

'In here, quickly.'

She stood beside an open door and pushed him inside. The door closed and he heard a key turn.

He was in a small room, lit only by a dirty window overhead; cluttered with empty boxes, cartons, crates and drums it was obviously used as a storeroom. He waited in the dusty gloom, listening, pushing fresh shells into his gun.

Feet echoed and a voice asked:

'The gringo – where is he?'

Paloma sounded annoyed.

'How should I know?'

He heard doors open as men searched, excited voices. Savage piled boxes one on another to reach the overhead window and climbed up. The platform was rickety and swayed and began to topple. He sweated; if he couldn't climb out he was trapped.

Someone rattled the doorhandle. A man's voice came.

'What's in here?'

Paloma said: 'Only a storeroom. It's kept locked.'

'Where's the key?'

103

'I suppose Carlos has it. Do you want me to bring it?'

'*Sí, señorita*, bring it immediately.'

Paloma called: 'Teresa,' and he heard their footsteps going away down the stairs.

Balanced carefully, Savage felt around the window frame with his fingertips; it seemed it should open – if it hadn't seized solid with age and the weather. He pushed upwards, and nothing happened. He pushed again, harder, and the platform of boxes moved under him.

A muffled voice came from the passage.

'Listen, I heard something.'

Savage waited. Footsteps moved away. He drew his Bowie and shoved the point between the edge of the window and the frame and dragged it around, hoping to loosen it. Dust and dirt crumbled away.

He put both hands under the frame and thrust up with all his strength. There was a sound like a rusty nail being withdrawn from old timber and the window lifted a fraction.

Hinges squealed as he forced it wide open. He pushed his shotgun out, then swung himself up and rolled over on to a flat roof, gasping with the effort, and breathless.

He took a few seconds to recover, and lowered the window, forcing it into place; he saw broken slabs of adobe and placed the largest across the frame to slow down any pursuers.

He looked about him. The roof next to the

cantina was lower and he dropped down easily. Then came a gap. He measured it by eye and took a running jump.

This was like old times in New York, travelling from rooftop to rooftop, exhilarating, and the memory brought a smile to his lips. He came to an outside stairway and raced down it, heading for the stable. Paloma and Teresa should already be there.

Now that he'd ordered his men upstairs after the gringo, Captain Rodrigo prudently waited below for news of his capture.

He'd only been thinking of celebrating his victory when he entered the cantina, after sending the lieutenant and his men after the few surviving bandits. He'd had no intention of sharing the glory. So it had been a shock to come face to face with Savage, reminding him that neither had he any intention of sharing the reward. Rodrigo had always done well by putting himself first.

He accepted another drink from Carlos and bought one for Ferdi, to console him for his loss. The dog-trainer was angry and depressed.

'If we take him alive, Ferdi, you shall have him to dispose of as you like.'

Ferdi grunted a monosyllable, looking towards the stairs. Rodrigo turned to see Paloma and her young sister coming down.

'Where do you think you're going?' he demanded.

The two girls watched Ferdi's remaining dog warily, but kept moving.

'You surely don't expect us to wait up there while your men are searching our rooms?'

They went out through a rear door and Rodrigo looked thoughtfully after them, a suspicion forming in his head. He called upstairs:

'Have you caught the gringo yet?'

'Not yet, *mi capitan*.'

Rodrigo made up his mind. He emptied his glass and called some of his men.

'You too, Ferdi. We'll take a look at the stable behind this cantina.'

They crossed the yard to the stable and he saw, beyond the open door, Paloma and Teresa saddling horses. Three horses, he noted, and smiled.

'Seize them,' he ordered. 'They have the Yanqui hidden somewhere.'

Teresa heard him and turned, drawing a small revolver.

'Murderer!' she screamed.

'Careful!' Paloma hissed. As two Rurales grabbed her sister, she whipped out a knife from under her skirt.

Rodrigo frowned. 'Beware! These kittens have claws.' A burly Rurale laughed and closed a big hand over hers, forcing her to drop the blade. She bit and kicked till she was subdued.

'This is one spitfire I shall enjoy taming, *Capitan*.'

Teresa tried to claw a captor's face with her fingenails, till she was overcome.

Rodrigo purred, 'It seems you were preparing to leave us – with the gringo, no doubt.'

He made a quick tour of the stable, peering behind bales of hay and sacks of corn, revolver in hand. He failed to find Savage and returned to his prisoners.

'Where is he?'

'Who?' Teresa asked, tongue in cheek.

He stared at her.

'I have not forgotten. You are the insolent one who claimed to win my race. We were interrupted last time, but I do not think that will happen again.'

He switched his attention to Paloma, regarding her with admiration.

'You are beautiful, *señorita*, and, I'm told, a fine dancer. It would be good if you danced for me and my men.'

Paloma gave him an icy look.

'I choose who I dance for!'

'But, of course.' Rodrigo smiled. 'Give me your whip, Ferdi.'

The dog-trainer held his last animal in check and passed the lash. Rodrigo took a firm grip and gave a flick of the wrist. The leather made a *crack*.

'I have not forgotten how . . . Turn the young girl to look at me.'

The Rurales manoeuvred Teresa around so she faced the captain. He smirked. 'I shall destroy her face first,' he announced, and raised the whip.

He paused briefly to stare at Paloma.

'Will you dance for my men? Or shall I remove the skin from this young one? You choose.'

Savage could hear voices as he crossed the yard to approach the stable and his gait changed to that of a big cat silently stalking his prey.

He could distinguish Rodrigo's voice, then Paloma's sharp 'Don't touch her!'

He peered around the edge of the open door, into the stable, and saw two Rurales gripping Paloma. Two more held Teresa prisoner, and the attention of everyone was on Rodrigo, about to strike with a whip.

Paloma, her face a shade paler, said:

'I'll do as you ask, *Capitan* – just leave her alone.'

Savage saw disappointment cloud Rodrigo's face; the captain *wanted* to use the whip. He studied the situation carefully.

Paloma was to one side. Rodrigo stood directly in front of Teresa, holding a whip. Behind him, Ferdi held the last of the killer dogs on a taut leash. The horses moved restlessly; they didn't like sharing quarters with the dog.

No one had noticed him yet, and he shifted position to get a clear view as he drew his Bowie. He judged the distance, took aim and threw.

The heavy blade pierced Ferdi's hand, the one holding the chain. He grunted with pain and relaxed his grip. Immediately the dog tore free and sprang at Rodrigo's back, bearing him to the ground. The captain screamed, once, and then slavering jaws snapped shut; the dog shook its head and ripped a lump of flesh from Rodrigo's neck.

Blood sprayed. A horse echoed his scream and reared and lunged to get away. Flailing hoofs scattered the Rurales as other horses imitated the first one in their panic.

He'd finally earned El Lobo's gold coins, Savage thought as he stepped forward, shotgun levelled. Ferdi started to move towards him, but checked himself as twin barrels pointed directly at his stomach.

The dog continued to feed as Savage reached forward and wrenched his knife from Ferdi's hand.

Teresa grabbed the reins of her horse and swung aboard. Paloma led Caesar and another horse outside. Savage backed out, pushing a shell into his shotgun. 'I hope nobody else wants to be a dead hero? Just freeze where you are while we leave.'

Ferdi's copper face became an emotionless mask.

'My dogs are dead, *El Capitan* is dead. When you cross into the land of the gringos, do not return.'

Savage nodded curtly and swung on to Caesar's back. He flicked the reins and trotted after Paloma and Teresa, out of town and towards the Rio Grande.

CHAPTER 12

RETURN TO EDEN

They splashed through swift-flowing water and climbed the riverbank to the track leading into Eden. Savage began to relax as they cantered along Main Street.

Paloma was instantly recognized and welcomed back with cheers; she flashed a professional smile at her admirers.

When they reached the livery, Marshal Dutton paused in the shoeing of a horse to stare.

'Doubted I'd see you again, Mr Savage. I guess you never caught up with El Lobo?'

Savage dismounted and stripped the saddle from Caesar.

'El Lobo is dead, Marshal, and I don't think he had much to do with Channing's murder.'

'That so?' Dutton doused hot iron in a bucket of water with a noise that sounded like a long sigh.

'Sure hope that doesn't mean you're going to stir up trouble again. Town and range have settled real quiet since you left us.'

'I'm not hunting trouble, Marshal. Just a meal, a bed and a night's undisturbed sleep.'

'That's fine by me.'

Teresa was stroking Caesar's muzzle and he seemed to like it.

'Will I ever race him again?' she asked wistfully.

'Why not? When I return him to the XL, I can mention that you won money on his back.'

Savage caught up his gear and walked Paloma to the Shamrock, then continued on to the hotel. He booked a bed and walked into the dining-room, ordered steak and coffee and watched the windows darken as evening clouds lowered.

The steak revived flagging energy but his muscles were still protesting; he sank another quart of coffee and retired to his room. A quick strip-wash and he was between the sheets and dreaming. . . .

A hand came out of the shadows, a hand that gripped a thin-bladed knife. Liquid darkness dripped from its point and he recognized Paloma's face above it. Her olive features rippled as if seen through moving water and changed into those of her sister. And changed again to an older face with big cheekbones.

It seemed important to put a name to this face and he struggled in his dream, breaking the

surface of consciousness, unsure whether he'd
heard a real scream or whether it were only part of
his dream.

He listened intently, heart beating faster. He
heard the strumming of a guitar, a quickening
rhythm, the stamping of shoe-heels. No scream;
but the dream had been vivid and lingered in his
mind.

A name nagged at him: Gladys Channing, and
he recalled Paloma's words: *Who else but a woman?
Someone close to him.*

Was it possible? Lying in the dark and staring at
the ceiling as if he might see the answer there, he
wondered why he hadn't suspected her before.
Tomorrow, he'd call on the widow and question
her. He dropped into a dreamless sleep.

Henry Horse sat on the corral fence and brooded.
It looked like the good times were over. He
watched his horses; it was habit to think of them as
his and he was depressed by the idea of leaving the
XL.

He preferred horses to humans. He preferred
almost any animal to men. He understood animals
where he often failed to understand the ways of his
own kind, except that they weren't his kind at all.

Henry vaguely remembered a lot of travelling in
his early days. Both his parents had been great travellers until his father was hanged as a horse-thief
and his mother settled into the tepee of a Crow
Indian.

After that, he'd travelled alone, making a living by breaking wild horses, a job that came naturally to him, moving on until he reached the XL and settled into a niche as the ranch wrangler.

That had been fine while he reported direct to the boss and maintained his freedom of action. But he'd never got on with the foreman. Wilson had something against travellers and regarded him as an outsider. As he had the Pinkerton . . . another outsider.

He thought briefly of Savage, and Caesar, and wondered how they were getting on. Waal, Caesar wouldn't let him down.

Time to move on again. Henry rolled a cigarette and smoked it slowly, considering his future. He smoked it down to a stub, threw it on the ground and stamped on it. Time to see the new boss; after all, moving on was his life.

He walked slowly towards the big house and, as he approached, heard voices. He recognized Wilson's, with his new boss, and paused with one foot on the bottom step of the veranda. Better to wait till the foreman had gone, he thought; he always avoided a confrontation when he could.

He didn't intend to listen, but the voices were raised at times and snatches of speech came to him. Not enough to make sense, but enough to make him feel uncomfortable. He didn't like what he heard and turned and walked quietly away. It was definitely time to move on.

*

Over breakfast, Savage considered how he might approach the new owner of the XL ranch. The widow might get the wrong idea.

Raised voices in the hotel dining-room suggested an answer.

'No, sir,' said an abrupt voice, 'I shall not renew your loan. I regret my weakness in lending you money in the first instance, and I shall not repeat that mistake. Now I would appreciate your leaving so that I may finish my breakfast in peace.' The speaker was a thin man, dressed in a dark suit, with a bald head.

'But Mr Adams—'

'No "buts", if you please. My mind is made up. Leave me in peace, or I shall complain to the management.'

'Goddamn you, Adams, you mangy skinflint! I hope the food poisons you and you roast in hell. I hope—'

A large man wearing an apron assisted the would-be borrower to leave the room and Savage thought: a banker is likely to know things about the XL that aren't generally known. But would he open up?

Savage sat back with another jug of coffee. He watched Adams leave and waited long enough to let him settle in his office. Then he crossed the street and spoke to the bank clerk.

'I guess it's known around town that I'm a Pinkerton. I'd like to talk with Mr Adams on a confidential matter if he can spare me a few minutes.'

'I'll ask him.'

When the clerk returned, he showed Savage into a small office at the back of the building.

Adams rose from a swivel chair to shake hands, then sat down again, using his desk as a shield. His manner was distant, his lips pressed into a bleak line; it would be as difficult to get words from him as money, Savage thought.

Adams stared at him.

'Well? I'm a busy man, so say what's on your mind.'

Savage was not tempted to risk a joke.

'I wondered if you have any doubts about the transfer of ownership of the XL property.'

The banker gave a snort like a small dog challenging a big one.

'Doubts? You're a bit late, aren't you? I recall that you hared off to Mexico after Mark Channing was murdered.'

'At that time, sir, there was a suspect I needed to question—'

'And now you've had second thoughts, is that it?' Adams' top lip curled. 'Mr Savage, you're too late. The deal has gone through.'

Savage's attention sharpened.

'What deal is that?'

'It *is* the XL property you're interested in?' Adams countered.

'Yes, and in particular Mrs Channing.'

'I repeat, you're too late. She sold the ranch immediately, accepting less than my valuation for a quick sale. Money has changed hands and she is now on her way East.'

Savage sat stunned. After a pause, he asked:

'D'you know where she's gone?'

'I don't have a forwarding address, if that's what you mean. The bulk of the money has been transferred to a Chicago bank. Is that all?'

'I guess it is.'

Savage rose as if dazed and, outside, wandered aimlessly. He had the feeling things were moving too fast for him to get a grip on. If there had been a telegraph office in Eden he might have wired the agency in Chicago to find her.

Was it worth the long ride to a bigger town where he could wire a message? He recalled her words: *I don't fancy spending the rest of my life in this place.*

There was one other place left to try: the emporium. Before he'd ridden south, he'd seen a display of Mexican knives on sale there. It was a long shot, but he retraced his steps.

As he walked through the doorway. the potbellied storekeeper winked at him.

'Get your man, Yank?'

Savage looked around the store and saw that nothing had changed. He nodded towards the display of knives.

'Did Mrs Channing ever buy one of these?'

'Mrs Channing? No, why should she? She rarely came here anyway.'

'Or anyone else from the XL?'

The storekeeper's expression changed.

'Why are you asking? Oh, no ... you're not pinning your murder on any of my customers! I don't have to answer your questions, so get out before I call the marshal.'

But he'd already said "no" about Gladys Channing before he became suspicious.

Savage said: 'Thanks, anyway,' and walked out, frustrated again. A client he'd been paid to protect had been killed and he didn't like the idea of the murderer getting away with his crime.

His feet carried him instinctively towards the livery stable, and a whinny from Caesar reminded him he should return the borrowed chestnut, though he was almost tempted to let Teresa have him. But he needed to talk to Henry Horse; some fresh information might have come to light since he'd left the ranch. With a nod to Dutton, he saddled up and rode away.

Beyond the limits of Eden, he turned Caesar loose, allowing him to set a fast pace; it might be the last gallop he'd get for a while.

The stallion responded by covering the ground like a four-legged machine, passing grazing longhorns and eating up the miles. The pounding rhythm was hypnotic and Savage was about half-way to the XL when he realized he hadn't asked for the identity of the new owner.

He swore, then shrugged mentally; he'd find out when he arrived. Further on he came across a small herd of cattle. who appeared lost on the open range; they huddled together, fat beef animals with short horns.

He was so used to seeing the lean Texan steers with their wide horns that he hauled back on the reins and stopped to look them over.

They were a different kind of animal from any he'd seen before, and he allowed Caesar to drift closer. They had been freshly branded XL, so the new owner was already making changes.

He was about to move on when he saw Wilson riding towards him, sided by two Texans.

The foreman scowled and tipped back his hat.

'What d'yuh want now? I thought I'd made it clear you ain't welcome.'

One of his riders laughed.

'Northerners can't ever understand they ain't wanted here.'

Savage regarded the foreman with a mild expression.

'I'm just returning a horse I borrowed. That's no cause for trouble, surely?'

'Yankees always cause trouble.'

'Maybe your new boss won't go along with that notion.'

'And maybe he will.' A light gleamed in Wilson's eyes. 'Suppose you get off'n your horse and start walking.'

Savage smiled. 'Guess I'll pick up my own cayuse from Henry first. I need to talk to him anyway.'

'Henry quit the XL. The new boss said he had to take orders from me, and he didn't like it.'

Wilson touched the butt of his revolver and glanced at the Texans.

'Does it look to you boys that this here Yankee was aiming to lift some of the boss's cattle?'

'Sure does, Willy,' one drawled, and raised his rifle.

Savage kicked Caesar's ribs and the stallion went forward in a rush; its shoulder rammed the foreman's mount and almost unseated him.

Savage let Caesar run. A rifle bullet winged close and the chestnut didn't like it. His ears flattened and he shot forward like an arrow from a bow.

Savage clung to the saddle horn, leaning down as low as he could, the way he'd seen Teresa ride; he doubted she could have got any more speed from the stallion. Caesar simply left their pursuers behind.

Henry had been right about this horse, though he'd meant escaping from Mexicans.

He reached the ranch before he reined back, and called: 'Halloo, the house!'

A slender figure stepped on to the veranda and Savage hardly recognized the dude he'd met in Eden. He saw the the same fair hair and blue eyes, but the whole bearing appeared different.

The face revealed lines and, dressed in a business suit, James Lacey no longer looked out of place in the West. He seemed very much a man in command of a large ranch.

'Mr Savage, this is a surprise. I hardly expected to see you again.' The words came easily.

And I never expected to see you here, Savage thought, like this. It was a shock and, for a moment, he wondered if the Englishman had a twin brother.

Wilson arrived in a hurry, almost falling out of the saddle; he looked furious.

'Let me handle this Yank, Mr Lacey. I caught him stealing our cattle!'

The dude coolly surveyed his foreman.

'I think not, Willy. I've spoken to you before about letting your temper get away from you. Step inside, Mr Savage.'

Wilson flushed and it looked as if he might go for his gun. 'But—'

'I said "No".' Suddenly there was iron in Lacey's voice, and Wilson turned away.

Inside, there had been alterations: comfortable armchairs, a bar at one end of the main room. It looked as if the XL might be turning into a dude ranch. Savage chose a hard-backed chair and sat down; he wanted explanations.

Lacey raised his voice and called for coffee. He sat in an armchair. He seemed pleasantly relaxed and, minutes later, a cowhand brought a jug of coffee and cups with saucers.

Savage said: 'I heard the XL had changed hands, but nobody thought to tell me you'd bought it.'

Lacey sipped coffee, and then smiled.

'If you think I own this place, you're imagining things. I've never been fortunate enough to have that kind of money.'

'And Mrs Channing?'

'Was happy to accept my offer. I fancy she'd had enough of the Wild West and yearned for bright lights and a taste of luxury.'

'Do you have an address for her?'

Something in Savage's tone made Lacey look sharply at him.

'Why? You can't suspect . . . Good Lord, I never thought . . . no, I can't believe that.'

Savage said flatly: 'I spoke to El Lobo' – Lacey raised an eyebrow – 'and I don't think he could get behind a man who didn't trust him and slip a knife into his back. But someone did.'

Lacey said slowly: 'I see the point you're making, and I suppose she's an obvious suspect, but I still don't believe it.'

'It has to be someone he trusted.'

'That makes sense, but . . .' Lacey paused, 'if I'd believed that, I'd never have dealt with her.'

He called for more coffee, and resumed when it came:

'I suppose I had better explain my own position here. I represent a syndicate of English business-men keen to buy into the cattle business in this country. I've been looking around for a suitable ranch since I arrived, and the XL suddenly became available. An excellent buy. I handled the deal for them and am now acting as manager until they appoint somebody permanent.'

'And Wilson?'

Lacey shrugged. 'Apart from his dislike of anyone from the North, he's an experienced foreman. I'm keeping him on to look after the day-to-day running of the ranch.'

'I noticed some very different cattle when I was riding here.'

'Yes, indeed – Herefords, an English breed. The syndicate is serious about importing superior stock to improve the herd by cross-breeding. This is only the start.'

Lacey seemed cool and in command. He indicated the changes in the house with a wave of his hand.

'For members of the syndicate when they visit. Naturally, they'll expect all the comforts of home.'

'I'm returning a horse I borrowed from your wrangler, Henry—'

'A pity about Henry. Apparently he dealt directly with Mr Channing, something I'm not prepared to do. When I pointed out that Wilson was the foreman and he should report to him, he left my employ. A personality clash there, I'm afraid.' Lacey made one of his old charming smiles. 'Keep the horse, Mr Savage.'

Savage frowned. Westerners valued horses and were reluctant to part with one.

'In Mexico, Paloma's sister, Teresa, won a race on Caesar. That animal may be worth something as a racer.'

'Paloma's sister? Really?' Lacey grinned, suddenly looking years younger. 'It might give me a chance with Paloma, I suppose – and I won't deny I have an itch there. But horse-racing is not what the XL is about.'

He came to his feet, obviously indicating that the interview was over, and this time he did not offer to shake hands.

As Savage left the house, he thought, but that doesn't explain *you*. The change was marked, and he wondered about James Lacey; there was little of the dude about him now.

CHAPTER 13

CAESAR'S NOSE

Wilson was not in sight when Savage stepped down from the veranda and walked towards the corral. But he didn't think the foreman had finished with him; he was just waiting for a time when his boss wasn't around to curb him.

The cowhand taking Henry's place was leaning on a fence, keeping one eye on his charges while he deftly spliced a rope.

'I left a rented horse with Henry,' Savage said.

The cowhand nodded. 'Only one horse here without our brand,' he said, and expertly cut out the animal.

'Sorry I missed Henry – I had no idea he was leaving.'

'Me neither, but not everyone gets on with Willy.'

'I reckon not,' Savage said, and took his time

124

walking the rented horse back to the veranda. He used his eyes but saw nothing obviously out of place.

He climbed aboard Caesar and set off towards Eden, leading his second mount. As he jogged along, he considered the XL foreman; was there more to his antagonism than a Southerner's hatred for anyone from the North? How far had Channing trusted Wilson? Did the Texan know something? It seemed likely – but how could he winkle it out of him?

Savage decided he'd stay over at Eden's hotel for a few days. Maybe he could figure a way to play Wilson like a fish on a line. Who knew what might surface?

When he reached town he turned in at the livery. Dutton was taking his ease in the sun, smoking his pipe, and his expression turned sour as Savage dismounted.

He took his pipe from his mouth and pointed the stem at him.

'I was hoping I'd seen the last of you. Let me warn you, the new owner of the XL is both liked and respected.'

Savage kept his tone light. 'I can't argue with that. Tell me about Henry Horse.'

'Henry?' The marshal sounded puzzled. 'What about Henry? I've no quarrel with him, nor has anyone else as far as I know. Keeps pretty much to himself.'

'It seems he quit the XL after a disagreement with Wilson.'

'That might not be so unusual as you think. Willy can be an awkward cuss if he takes a dislike to you. But this news surely surprises me – I'd have thought Henry was a fixture there.'

'Seems not.' Savage picked up his shotgun and saddle-bags and headed along the boardwalk. Obviously Dutton hadn't seen the wrangler since he quit. He walked into the emporium.

The storekeeper looked stonily at him.

'You again?'

'Just a friendly enquiry. Which way did Henry Horse go when he left?. I'm guessing he stocked up here before travelling.'

The storekeeper muttered something under his breath.

'I ain't seen Henry lately, and he didn't outfit himself here.'

'Just asking,' Savage said, and walked outside.

After a meal at the hotel – and Henry wasn't staying there – he looked in at the Shamrock. Mike called:

'Will you take that drink with me now?'

'Why not? Make it a small beer. What I came to ask is, have you seen Henry Horse lately?'

'Not for a while, now you mention it.' Mike placed a glass on the counter in front of Savage. 'And this is a regular port of call any time he hits town, so I guess he's not in.'

Savage nodded and sipped his beer. He wondered how far Channing had trusted Henry. The wrangler had handed over Caesar with no

126

difficulty – to get rid of him? Something didn't feel right.

He watched Paloma perform her dance routine. When she finished she brushed against him, deliberately spilling his drink as she headed for the stairs.

'Are you in the mood for some loving tonight?' she murmured.

'Surely,' he said, and then spotted an old-timer sitting alone at a table with an empty glass. 'I'll be up in ten minutes.'

Lacey watched from the window as Savage walked towards the corral. He wasn't worried, but he was thoughtful. Savage wasn't some hick Westerner; he was a detective and from New York. Well, he would wait and see what developed, if Willy managed to control himself. The foreman had an unfortunate habit of doing the wrong thing before he'd worked out what was needed.

He crossed to the bar, poured himself a generous measure of brandy and settled in a comfortable armchair. At ease, his mind drifted back some months to a coffee house on Cheapside in the City of London, England. That too, had been a time of waiting.

A resting actor did a lot of waiting, and not all of it for a theatre call. He'd long since signed on with an employment agency providing services for well-to-do families, and could play a gentleman's manservant to perfection.

He sat in a booth with a high back where he could watch the doorway, and listen to any conversation in the booth behind. He sometimes picked up useful information that way.

He sipped coffee and watched the street. A horse-drawn coal-cart lumbered by; a few pedestrians scurried beneath umbrellas. It was only a drizzle of rain but seemed to form a damp grey mist that hung like a veil over the far side of the street; at least, he thought, it laid the soot.

A bell tinkled as the glass-panelled door opened and an urchin with red hair came in. He held a folded sheet of notepaper and made straight for him.

'Ain't you the lucky one, Jim.'

Lacey broke the seal, read the note and handed the boy a threepenny bit.

'Just say I'll take it, and get me a cab.'

The urchin darted outside. Lacey followed at a more sedate pace; getting into his role as butler to Sir John required a show of dignity, and by the time he reached the pavement a horse-drawn cab was waiting. 'Where to, sir?'

'Fetter Lane, and I'll need you to wait. I have to go out again.'

At his lodgings, Lacey shaved and changed into a black pin-stripe and starched collar before descending to the street.

'Bedford Square, and go by way of Aldwych.'

'Aye, sir.'

The horse leaned forward, the wheels turned and the cab started off wih a jerk.

Lacey sat upright, eyes bright with anticipation, looking out as they passed a theatre he'd once played. He gave the doorman a friendly nod. Of course, he'd hoped for a part in this new play . . . but now he had something else, and was excited. Sir John was reputed to have irons in more than one fire.

At Bedford Square his employer was abrupt.

'This is a private meeting, Lacey, and anything you overhear is confidential. My own man is away and, if you do the job right, there may be something more for you.'

Lacey had played a butler on stage more than once. This current role went smoothly; he was politely welcoming, discreet and self-effacing; drinks were waiting and there were sandwiches on a sideboard. Time passed effortlessly, as it always did when he was into a role.

The meeting ended and the guests departed.

Sir John was smiling when he invited him into his study.

'Well done, Lacey. My associates are not idiots, yet no one challenged you on any point. They accepted you in the part you played. Sit down. A drink? Cigar?'

Lacey's pulse quickened as he realized this job had been some kind of test.

'I know you're an actor-Johnny. I have interests in the theatre – and the agency you sometimes work for – and I've seen you on stage in several very different parts.'

Lacey tensed; the real job was about to be revealed. Sir John made himself comfortable. He lit a cigar, sipped his brandy.

'Now then, James, do you think you could handle the role of an aristocrat? Not here, on their own turf, but abroad. Out West in fact, in what used to be called our colonies. Perhaps even further west. . . .'

Teresa pleaded, 'Let me exercise him, please.'

'Not today,' Savage said, tightening a strap. 'I'm expecting to cover a lot of territory.'

Caesar looked from one to the other, restlessly shifting his hoofs; it didn't matter to him who was on his back, he just wanted to run.

Teresa sniffed. She knew Savage had slept in her sister's bed last night, and disapproved; but he'd got them out of Nuevo Eden and a stable much like this one.

She gave a heavy sigh to make sure her sacrifice was noticed.

'Oh, I can wait.'

Dutton, filling his pipe by the anvil, watched and listened, a smile curving his lips.

He figured maybe a couple of years and this young one would be taking over from Paloma as far as the boys were concerned.

Savage got in the saddle, checked his shotgun and Bowie and picked up the reins. He touched his hat and rode out of the stable and out of town.

He let the chestnut run until he was out on his own, away from the river and the main herds. He paused to look back; no one seemed interested in following him.

He took a sheet of paper from his pocket and studied it. The old-timer in the Shamrock had sketched a rough map of the XL range in exchange for a couple of drinks. The range covered a vast area and it wasn't all grass; to the north-west was semi-desert, scrub and brush. He headed that way.

When he saw riders moving cattle in the distance he angled away, not wanting to talk to anyone at the moment. He rode on after stopping to consult the map again, noting the position of the ranch house in relation to this increasingly barren area. He set a slow pace, watching the ground for tracks. If Henry Horse had travelled this way he must have left some sign of his passage.

He came across few hoof-prints, and those old, until he found recent sign of two horses riding side by side. Henry and. . . ?

Further on the tracks disappeared beneath hoof-marks denoting the passage of a herd. Cattle here? It seemed unlikely.

He cast around in widening circles until Caesar became restless, and he remembered the old-timer's advice: *When in doubt, let your horse do the thinking.*

He gave a flick of the reins, sat back and let

Caesar follow his nose. The stallion chose a narrow gulch lined with scrub, moving slowly at first and gradually quickening pace. Presently he stopped and lowered his head and shoved at some loose brush, disturbing a cloud of flies. There was a man's body and Caesar nosed at a shirt pocket.

Savage dismounted and hauled Caesar back, giving him sugar-lumps from his own pocket. He raised his neckerchief to cover his mouth and nostrils because the corpse was beginning to smell.

Predators had already found the body but there was enough left to recognize the missing wrangler. He peered closely until he was sure: Henry had been shot.

CHAPTER 14

A MATTER OF LOYALTY

Savage stepped back, lowered his neckerchief and took in several long draughts of fresh air. The idea that Henry Horse might have had something to do with Channing's death had crossed his mind; he dismissed it now.

Who had shot him? Why? Had the wrangler found out something that meant he had to be silenced? At least this gave him a new line of enquiry.

He remounted Caesar and headed for the ranch. The stallion still wanted to run and knew the way home; he covered the ground at a gait that destroyed distance. Savage pulled back on the reins as he approached the house, but the only sign of life was the new man working on a corral fence.

He called: 'Did you see Henry leave? Was anyone with him?'

'I didn't – and no idea. I didn't get this job till after he'd gone.'

Savage hitched Caesar to the veranda, went up the steps and pushed open the door.

'Anyone home?'

Lacey's voice came from a back room.

'Who is it? Can it wait?'

'Savage. I have some news.'

'If you'll wait a couple of minutes, I'll be with you.'

Savage waited, and then heard the scrape of a chair being pushed back. Lacey appeared, pushing a hand through his hair.

'Paperwork,' he said, making a rueful expression. 'It's my first time for managing a ranch and I have to make a showing. What's the news?'

Savage watched him carefully.

'I remember you told me Henry Horse left after a clash with your foreman.'

'A personality clash. I didn't intend to imply bad blood.'

'Did Henry leave alone?'

'I don't know – I didn't see him leave.'

'Who might have seen him?'

'I've really no idea.'

Lacey was stonewalling, so Savage changed tactics.

'Is Wilson around? I have some questions for him.'

'He's out on the range somewhere. Questions about what, exactly?'

'I found Henry's body. He's been shot.'

James Lacey stood still; his hands slowly clenched. He didn't speak immediately, but the expressions shifting across his face suggested he was trying out possible comments without finding one he liked.

Savage waited. Then he felt something hard and cold touch the back of his neck.

Wilson rode back towards the XL ranch house in an uncertain frame of mind. He rode alone, and his face under the flat black hat was like a dark cloud because he was a man of certainties.

Certain he was right. Certain that Texans were superior to other men, especially Northerners; he had a special hatred for them because as a rebel he'd fought them during the war.

He'd known where he was with Mr Channing. They had an understanding: Texans on top, greasers a pain in the arse.

But with Channing gone (the widow woman didn't count) and a new boss he found himself in a world of uncertainties and he didn't like it a bit.

At first he'd despised the English dude, but since buying the XL Lacey, too, had changed – and Wilson didn't want change. There was already more than enough change going on around him –

homesteaders moving in and the younger men pushing aside their elders. It was enough to make a saint uncertain.

The boss puzzled him. He didn't know anything about ranching but he was already introducing a new breed – foreign cattle – into the herd. He figured Lacey for a hollow man, a sham, and was aiming to talk him out of that nonsense.

Wilson clung to the one true fact of life; a man was loyal to his outfit, and his outfit was the XL. That was the only thing that mattered, even if some of the younger men didn't see it that way.

He'd been suspicious, but suspicions counted for nothing. Channing represented the past and the past had gone for ever; the XL carried on.

It hadn't seemed credible at first and Lacey, when challenged, admitted nothing, just smiled that bland smile of his. So it was unfortunate that Henry had overheard, but he'd dealt with Henry. There would be no rumours from that source.

But when he'd returned to tell the boss not to worry, that his little problem had been taken care of, Lacey had not been pleased. So? Wilson gave a mental shrug; only the XL mattered, not any one individual.

Of course, there was still that New York spy poking his nose in where it wasn't wanted, and he wondered why Lacey hesitated. It would be the easiest thing in the world to make Savage disappear. So why not? Doubts seemed to spring up like weeds and Wilson was a troubled man.

He reached the corral, stepped down from his saddle and handed the reins to the new wrangler. The cowhand said:

'Mr Savage is back, talking with the boss.'

'That so?' Wilson kept his voice casual, but he hitched his gunbelt higher and loosened his revolver in its holster as he walked towards the house.

He moved quietly up the steps of the veranda, and paused, listening. The door was half-open and he heard voices inside.

'Is Wilson around? I have some questions for him.'

A Northern accent told him it was Savage speaking, and he smiled coldly. Closer than you think . . .

'He's out on the range somewhere. Questions about what exactly?'

It doesn't matter what it's about, Wilson thought, lifting his revolver from its holster. This answers all questions.

'I found Henry's body . . .'

Did you now? That's your bad luck. Wilson moved like a shadow, Indian-style, towards Savage's voice, aiming to get behind him.

'. . . he's been shot.'

Big surprise. Wilson kept moving closer.

Lacey remained silent, facing Savage. Obviously he could see him now, but his face revealed nothing.

Wilson was surprised. Lacey's face was a mask

that showed little of what he must be feeling. He closed the gap, holding his breath.

He touched the back of Savage's neck with his levelled Colt.

'Don't even think it.'

Savage froze.

'Good boy. Now throw the shotgun away.'

Savage obeyed, and Wilson used his free hand to snatch the Bowie from its sheath. He tossed the knife to Lacey, who caught it neatly.

'Your weapon, I think,' Wilson drawled. 'Do you want to stick him, or shall I shoot him?'

'For God's sake, no!' Lacey suddenly showed the tension he was under. 'He's not one man on his own – he belongs to the Pinkerton organization. If he goes missing, a whole bunch of them will descend on us.'

'You running scared of some damned Yankees?'

'No, I'm not. This has to look like an accident – surely you can see that? That's only common sense.'

Wilson just looked at him.

'You're too impetuous, Willy – you shouldn't have shot Henry. Think first, perform later would be a useful rule to follow.'

'Like this?'

Wilson lifted his Colt and smashed it down, hard, on Savage's skull. He watched with satisfaction as the Yankee spy crumpled like a discarded sack.

*

Paloma tried not to scream at her sister, but her temper was rising and threatened to boil over. She'd got up late, her bed was still rumpled from the night and all she really wanted was to sip her coffee quietly. Teresa had probably eaten a full breakfast and was bursting with energy. It appeared she had already been to the livery.

She'd burst into her room above the Shamrock's bar, moaning about Savage going off on his horse. She seemed to miss the point that it was his horse and not hers.

'It's not fair,' she bawled, and Paloma rolled her eyes towards the ceiling. 'I should be up on Caesar, winning money for us. He really should let me—'

Paloma flared up.

'Stop this nonsense at once! If Father could hear you now he'd be ashamed. Disgusted! A daughter of El Lobo should not indulge in such childish stupidity. What's wrong with you? Are you sickening for something? Or just in love? Stop behaving like a spoilt child!'

Teresa paused, her mouth open, and Paloma went on:

'Of course it's not fair! What idiot told you it was? You're old enough to have learnt that nothing is ever fair in this world. Grow up!'

Each sister glowered at the other.

'Now leave me alone,' Paloma snapped. 'You know I'm not at my best in the morning. You've got a horse – why don't you ride that?'

Teresa's mouth closed like a trap. She turned on a heel and went out, slamming the door after her.

CHAPTER 15

A DAUGHTER OF EL LOBO

His head ached. His arms and legs felt numb. He was moving. After a while memory asserted itself; Wilson had been behind him, so he was the one who'd knocked him out. He promised himself a return match in the near future.

Another while passed before he realized he was tied to a horse crossing the prairie, a prisoner. He heard Wilson cursing the horse that carried him and guessed he was on Caesar; the stallion objected to being led by a rope tied to another rider's saddle horn.

He drifted in and out of consciousness until Lacey's voice came:

'I think he's awake.'

'Not for long,' Wilson said, and swore again.

'This goddamned useless horse – it's a good job we're getting rid of it.'

Savage watched the ground go by, the grass thinning and browning; they were headed into a barren area, and he could expect no help here.

Lacey jogged alongside, chatting easily.

'You're an embarrassment, you know. If only you'd had the good sense to report that El Lobo killed Channing, and that El Lobo was dead, we wouldn't have had all this trouble.'

Caesar tried to break away and Wilson quirted him. Lacey waited for the chestnut to settle before he went on:

'You see, Channing refused to sell and I was getting desperate – there were not many ranches of the size required, and the XL was ideal. I had a limit set for expenses and time, by the syndicate, and I was pretty sure I could persuade his wife to sell.'

Savage was only half-listening; he was working at the knots on the ropes around his wrists, but it was hopeless without any feeling in his fingers. He succeeded only in breaking a fingernail.

'Channing, of course, wasn't afraid of a silly-ass dude. I've found Westerners easy to fool – give them the type of English gentleman they expect . . .' Lacey smirked '. . . and they fool themselves.'

'On stage I found it easy enough – the blade simply slid into the handle. I was surprised to find it no more difficult in real life. The blade went in and Channing collapsed. Easy!'

'Just like you,' Wilson told Savage, and laughed.

He hauled on the reins and they stopped in the middle of an expanse of empty range.

'This'll do.' He dismounted, showing Savage the blade of his own Bowie.

Savage waited calmly. Lacey hadn't gone to this trouble to let his foreman carve his initials on him.

Wilson flourished the knife threateningly, then slashed the ropes holding him. Savage slipped sideways and hit the ground. Wilson slammed a boot into him, and again.

You're a dead man, Yankee!'

He raised his quirt and lashed Caesar. The horse squealed and bolted.

'Whoever finds this useless animal is welcome to him – guess they'll assume you came off. Too bad.'

Savage struggled to get upright, but the rope had been so tight the circulation in his limbs had been ruined. Wilson sneered as he flopped back, unloaded the shotgun and dropped it beside him. He stuck the Bowie back in its sheath.

Lacey surveyed him, satisfied.

'No one's going to be able to tell what state he was in before . . .'

'Before he becomes mincemeat,' Wilson finished. 'But just to make sure . . .'

He raised his revolver again. Savage tried to dodge but his reaction was too slow. The barrel crashed down on his skull and he blacked out. . . .

*

The ground trembled and shook and his teeth vibrated in sympathy. An earthquake? In a half-daze he seemed to hear wild shouting, and then shooting. It was the gunfire that snapped him back to reality; it spoke of danger.

He forced himself to stand, and found that he had some use of his arms and legs, although his movements were painfully slow.

He stared about him, alone on the open range with hard-baked earth and stones and sparse brown grass. There was no sign of Caesar. In the distance a cloud of dust blotted out the horizon and he heard a fast drumming of hoofs.

Someone was driving a herd, frightening them into a stampede and aiming them at him. Wilson and Lacey would be safe behind the cattle, urging them on, but he was out in front and at risk of being trampled. Which must be what they intended.

He hobbled about like a cripple, testing his legs. He picked up the shotgun; empty. He still had his knife, but that wouldn't save him from goring horns and sharp hoofs.

He couldn't run far, or fast enough to escape. The cattle were runaways, almost impossible to stop, bunched up and heading straight for him, driven by a foreman who knew what he was doing. Despite the sun he felt cold; yet sweat rolled off him.

He was looking at death and seeing no way out. Until he recalled the story Teresa had told of the

Mexican hero, the *vaquero*, whose horse had fallen before a stampede.

He didn't really believe it, but he grabbed at this one-in-a-thousand chance. He fumbled in his pocket. Wilson had been too sure of himself and hadn't searched him. He brought out two shells from a handful and loaded the gun.

He waited, legs quivering as the ground shook, watching the swaying heads and horns. Their eyes seemed glazed and he doubted they were even aware of him as they charged, legs pounding up and down.

He stood braced, judging distance, calculating time. He marked the leader, head down and horns levelled like twin spears. Perhaps it saw him as a challenge and came directly at him, as large and as fast as a locomotive. He knew he would have only the one shot before he was pounded flat. He took a long breath and held it, shotgun aimed; he flexed his trigger finger.

There was no more shooting, or shouting, from behind the herd. Neither Lacey nor Wilson would want to be seen anywhere near the scarred earth of a stampede.

The front wave of animals was almost on top of him. He concentrated. *Now.* He triggered both barrels and the gun bucked in his hands.

It seemed nothing changed as he stood waiting, helpless but hopeful . . . and then the leading steer's front legs buckled under it.

It stumbled and skidded along, horns gouging

145

the ground. Momentum carried it forward until it slid to a halt in front of him.

Savage dropped between the horns, huddling close to the bloody snout so that he seemed to form part of the dead animal.

The herd parted to go around their fallen leader and closed ranks again, ignoring him. The noise was frightening; hoofs hitting the baked ground like thunder, horn clashing against horn, a terrified bellowing as the steers ran in panic.

Savage was quickly coated in dust, and choking, until he worked his neckerchief up over his face. He closed his eyes. The smell sickened him. His whole body shook in time with the trembling of the earth as maddened cattle passed on each side of him.

He waited, counting off seconds. The herd swept by until the last animal had gone and, gradually, the air grew still and silent. He found the silence restful, and it was some minutes before he staggered to his feet.

As the dust began to settle, he moved a little way off from the dead steer and banged the dirt from his clothes. His shirt was stained by the animal's blood, but the sun was shining as he took in a lungful of air. Suddenly it felt good to be alive.

Lacey and Wilson had had their turn; now it was his. He fished two more shells from his pocket and reloaded the shotgun; he checked that his Bowie was still in its sheath.

He looked at the sun to get a bearing and, at a

stumbling walk, lurched in the direction of the ranch house.

Fuming, Teresa clattered down the stairs of the Shamrock like a herd of angry buffalo. She glowered at passers-by as she stamped along Eden's boardwalk. There were times when her sister was a pain in the neck. Just that she was older didn't give her the right to speak to her like that. It wasn't fair!

At the livery, Marshal Dutton looked the other way and kept silent; he'd seen Teresa in a temper before. He ignored her as she slapped a saddle on her horse, vaulted aboard and charged out.

She rode hard and fast; the horse that had once carried the Grey Ghost was another that liked to run. The ride was exhilarating. With a horse under her, the sun and the wind soon changed her mood. Her head cleared; maybe Paloma was right – after all, she was a daughter of El Lobo!

She reined back to study her surroundings: away from the river, on open range and close to the barrens.

She saw a few exhausted cattle and her curiosity was aroused. Should she investigate? Or turn back? She was reluctant to return and, anyway, Paloma had told her to ride her horse.

She went forward again, alert, and saw a riderless horse in the distance. Maybe someone had come off? She urged her mount on, veering towards the stray; it looked her way and then trotted towards her. She recognized Caesar and wondered what had happened to Savage.

She scanned the horizon but saw no one. Caesar nosed at her pocket and she realized she'd left without any sugar-lumps. She could have kicked herself, but that was Paloma's fault.

'Find him,' she said. 'Find him, and you'll find sugar.'

Caesar moved off and she followed. Something was wrong; Mr Savage was not the sort of man to fall off. Further on the ground was chewed up by the hoofs of a herd travelling at speed, and she began to worry. If he'd come off in front of stampeding cattle his chance of survival was low.

She searched, but saw no sign of him, and followed Caesar till she came to a dead steer; one that had been shotgunned. Now Caesar forged ahead.

She pushed her horse to a gallop, following after the stallion. The sun was beginning its nightly slide towards the horizon, and soon it would be dark. Then she saw a figure on foot ahead of her, limping and swaying from side to side and carrying a shotgun.

CHAPTER 16

FINAL PERFORMANCE

There was a taste of dust in his throat, and a drum was beating a slow tattoo in his head. Savage kept putting one foot in front of another, but the tracks he left zigzagged like those of a drunk.

He had one fixed idea that he clung to; he was going to reach the XL ranch and deal with the pair who had failed to kill him. He intended to make sure they never had a second chance. He resented being made to look a fool.

He lurched on, vaguely aware that the air was cooler and the sun lower in the sky. After a time-less interval he became conscious of hoofbeats and turned, lifting his shotgun.

One rider, two horses. He covered them until he recognized Teresa following Caesar. The stallion snorted as he approached and started to nuzzle at his shirt pocket.

The young Mexican girl said:

'I promised him sugar-lumps if he found you.'

Savage searched his pocket; the lumps were crushed and bloody but the chestnut accepted them with greedy satisfaction. His saddle-bags were still in place, and he grabbed his water bottle, rinsed out his mouth and drank. He began to feel better.

'Thanks,' he croaked. He pulled out some jerky and chewed on it and felt the strength flow back into his limbs.

'So what happened?' Teresa demanded.

'It was Lacey – the dude – who murdered Channing. When the wrangler caught on, Wilson shot him. They fooled me and aimed to bury me under a herd of cattle – and might have succeeded if you hadn't told me about your *vaquero*.'

Her eyes bulged.

'It really worked? I wish I'd seen that!' She regarded him critically. 'Even if you do look a wreck, you're sure a hard man to stop.'

'And now I'm going to see they don't murder anyone else.'

'What can I do?' she asked eagerly.

Savage stared at her: still young enough to be considered almost a child, yet experienced in the ways of survival. He decided she could help, and nodded.

'This. Rustle some XL cattle just before dawn.

Take those closest to the house, and make plenty of noise. Lure the cowhands away for me.'

Teresa gurgled with laughter.

'So, a lawman is inviting a daughter of El Lobo to help herself to Texan cows – I must get Paloma in on this. *Adios*!' She wheeled her horse about and galloped away.

Savage made a fuss of Caesar till she was out of sight. There was no hurry now, and he'd grown fond of this horse. He swung into the saddle and Caesar went forward as eager as ever to be on the move. He took a roundabout route to avoid any night guards.

He had only the vaguest idea for a plan of attack, preferring to decide on the spot, at the time; but it would help if Teresa separated Lacey and Wilson from the XL hands.

The darkness was silvered by moonlight as he dismounted and left the chestnut to graze. He checked his shotgun and Bowie and approached the house on foot. No lights showed, and the still air reverberated with snores from the bunkhouse.

His immediate objective was to get on to the roof of the ranch house without being heard. From there he would be hard to get at and would have a commanding position.

The house was built of timber and, as he knew from experience, boards creaked. He moved cautiously around the house, noting the kitchen door at the rear, and ducking down as he passed a window. He found what he was looking for: a water

151

barrel with a cover. He tested it and found it secure.

Getting up was not easy; his hard-used muscles had still not fully recovered but, eventually, he hoisted himself on top of the barrel.

Standing upright, he could just reach the parapet. He pushed his shotgun up and over the edge, and then swung himself up. The roof was flat with a gentle slope towards the back; he lay still, recovering his breath and listening. No one stirred.

He rolled over and looked out above the parapet; he had a clear view all around and the element of surprise. He cradled his shotgun and waited for sunrise.

Perhaps he half-dozed, because he was roused by distant shouts; voices calling back and forth in Spanish. Teresa and Paloma were at work. Hoofbeats echoed and cows bawled as they began to run.

First light tinted the horizon the colour of a blood-orange, and dust began to rise. The air quivered with the bellowing of steers who objected to moving before they were ready. He made out the shadowy figures of riders lashing the animals' hides with quirts. For only two young women they created a satisfying level of noise.

A shout went up from the bunkhouse:

'*Rustlers!*'

Half-dressed cowhands came out, cursing and strapping on gunbelts as they ran to the corral for horses. Saddles were slapped on in a hurry.

Wilson was the last one to show, fully dressed. He shouted:

'Get after them. I'll tell the boss, and follow yuh.'

One by one the cowhands galloped off, and Savage smiled; he didn't think they'd catch Paloma or Teresa.

He looked down the twin barrels of his shotgun, lined up on Wilson's black hat, and waited for him to move closer. He watched, step by step, and then called softly:

'Willy.'

Wilson paused and looked around, puzzled.

'Up here!'

The foreman's head tilted upwards and he looked into the double-bore. Despite the shock, he reacted fast. His hand jerked a revolver free of its holster and triggered it.

Savage felt the lead pass close and lovingly squeezed both triggers, aiming at the foreman's eyes.

Wilson went over backwards, screaming and clawing at his face.

James Lacey smiled in his sleep. He was dreaming of success. He stood alone on the stage, the cast behind him, the limelight concentrated on him. He bowed to an audience giving him a standing ovation; an audience that stretched, row on row, further back than he could see.

Loud clapping and wild cheering showed that

his merit had been recognized, that never again would he lack a wealthy patron, that producers would come to him. He dreamed of a future where the world was his stage.

Of course, he already had plenty to be pleased about. Channing had been almost too easy, and Mrs Channing a pleasure to manipulate. He felt superior to these barely literate Westerners, and the death of Savage removed the last threat to his security.

Noises off intruded. Crude swearing, the bawling of cattle being moved along. Then, much closer, a shouted alarm: 'Rustlers!' The word had a penetrating quality and he frowned, half-awake. Horses galloping. Wilson's voice, 'I'll tell the boss . . .'

He got out of bed in a hurry and began to dress; he couldn't afford to forget he had a part to play as the ranch-manager. Through the window he glimpsed Wilson striding towards him and, from somewhere, heard a voice he'd never expected to hear again.

'Up here!'

It sounded like Savage's voice and had the effect of a deluge of cold water. Suddenly he was wide awake. That wasn't possible, was it?

Savage had been trampled into the earth, so he couldn't be threatening anyone now. Lacey was sure ghosts coming back to haunt murderers only happened in bad plays. He must still be dreaming . . . then he remembered he'd admitted to the

Pinkerton that he'd knifed Channing, and began to sweat.

He heard the sharp *crack* of a revolver and the roar of a shotgun. Wilson's face dissolved into pulp and he went down, screaming and whimpering.

Appalled, Lacey turned away, feeling sick. This wasn't a dream; neither was it a stage death where the corpse got up and walked when the curtain came down. Wilson was dead, and he was alone.

Just the idea of facing Savage unmanned him and he stood shaking. Concentrate! Imagine! Savage had to be silenced somehow, anyhow. Paralysis gripped him, worse even than the time he forgot his lines and dried up at a crucial moment. Think! But all his brain conjured up were scenes from a melodrama he'd played early in his career.

He remembered the villain's come-uppance when he perished in a fire he'd started himself . . . *fire!* The house was built of timber, it was dry and Savage was on the roof, ideally placed for a funeral pyre. This was his cue.

He stopped shaking and moved with calm deliberation to the kitchen. He saw everything he needed: a kerosene-lamp, old fat in a frying-pan, a newspaper. He smashed the lamp against the timber wall. Matches. He looked around; somewhere there must be . . . Yes! His fingers fumbled, broke the first match.

He struck another; it sparked and fizzled out. He made a spill of paper and fired it with his third, careful strike.

The paper flamed and he touched it to the kerosene-soaked timber. The wall flared up quickly. The fat started to melt and burn and a foul-smelling smoke erupted in a dense cloud. Choking, he moved to the back door and opened it to get a through draught. A sudden wave of heat acted as a prompt.

Exit, pursued by a tongue of flame.

Savage reloaded and watched Wilson till he stopped twitching. One down and one to go; now, where was Lacey?

He heard nothing from below as he moved quietly across the flat roof; the Englishman might try to escape by the back door, or a window, if he'd seen what happened to his foreman.

He glanced towards the horizon, but there was no sign of the XL hands returning. He sniffed the air: something burning? Was Lacey cooking breakfast? The idea amused him and, as his mouth began to water, he was tempted to drop in for a meal.

Then he realized the fire was more serious than that. He heard a crackle of flames below as smoke drifted up.

He smiled bleakly; Lacey was aware of him and trying to burn him to death while he hid behind a wall of smoke. Did the Englishman imagine he'd jump, and then be waiting for him?

Lacey couldn't stay inside a burning house for long; he'd be driven out to make a run for it.

Savage decided to wait him out.

The smoke thickened, obscuring his view. Waves of hot air wafted up, driving him back from the parapet. Red and yellow flames flickered below. A wall started to collapse and part of the roof sagged. Dust and ash rose with the stink of smoke and started him coughing.

He felt poised on the brink of hell with an incandescent glow below waiting to incinerate him. It was too easy to imagine the fall. . . .

The soles of his boots were scorched and his feet uncomfortably hot. He'd need to jump soon, but where was Lacey? It was more difficult to see anything but burning timber, or hear anything above the roar of the fire. He kept moving, straining his ears and eyes – and then he glimpsed a man-shape through the swirling smoke: *Lacey*!

He ignored the pain from burns and blisters, dropped his shotgun over the side and drew his Bowie. Hiding in a pall of smoke was something two could do.

He ignored the flames, stood poised on the parapet nearest his quarry, and jumped.

He landed behind the XL manager, glimpsed his shadowy form through a swirl of smoke and stalked him. He saw Lacey's back, the way he must have seen Channing's, an obvious target, and moved up on him with Indian stealth.

The blade of the Bowie went in with his full strength behind it, sliding between bones to reach the heart, and came out dripping blood.

'Now you really appreciate how easy it is,' he murmured.

Lacey exhaled a faint sigh and sank to the ground, giving his final performance.

Savage wiped the blade on his shirt and sheathed it. He picked up his shotgun and, hair singed and clothes smouldering, limped away from the ruined ranch house.